This book belongs to:

Be Bad

PRAISE FOR VILLAINS ACADEMY

'A charmingly villainous adventure about
friendship, school and unspeakable evil.'
Louie Stowell, author of *Loki: A Bad God's Guide to Being Good*

'Frightfully fun – *Villains Academy* had me
cackling from the very first page!'
Katie Tsang, co-author of the Dragon Realm series

'A joyful hug of a book with genuine warmth and heart.'
Hannah Gold, author of *The Last Bear*

'I loved the spookily funny *Villains Academy*.
It's a work of (evil) genius!'
Jenny McLachlan, author of *The Land of Roar*

'Criminally fun!'
Danny Wallace, author of *The Day the Screens Went Blank*

'Heart-warming and hilarious – *Villains Academy* is a spookalicious
treat, set to terrify every other book on your shelf.'
Jack Meggitt-Phillips, author of *The Beast and the Bethany*

'An absolute HOOT! Evil laughs aplenty!'
Sophy Henn, author and illustrator of the Pizazz series

'A delightfully fun adventure with real heart and humour.'
Benjamin Dean, author of *Me, My Dad and the End of the Rainbow*

'Immersive, funny, and with a cast of scarily loveable characters,
Villains Academy made me feel like I was IN the book!'
Mel Taylor-Bessent, author of *The Christmas Carrolls*

'This is a brilliant, bonkers work packed with top-notch illustration.'
Jack Noel, author and illustrator of the Comic Classics series

'Full of wonderful characters, *Villains Academy* is such a FUN read!'
Rikin Parekh, illustrator of The Worst Class in the World series

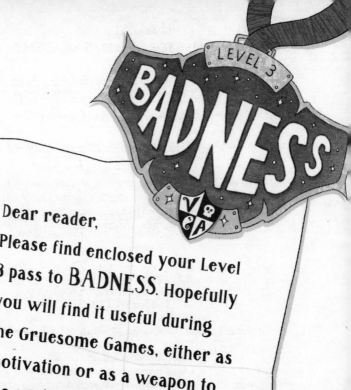

Dear reader,

Please find enclosed your Level 3 pass to BADNESS. Hopefully you will find it useful during the Gruesome Games, either as motivation or as a weapon to use against your enemies.

P.S. There are no rules from here on in ... Proceed with caution.

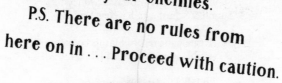

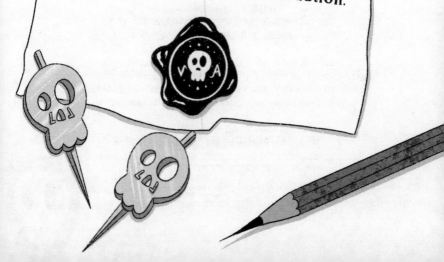

First published in Great Britain in 2024 by Simon & Schuster UK Ltd

Copyright © 2024 Ryan Hammond

1 3 5 7 9 10 8 6 4 2

Simon & Schuster UK Ltd
1st Floor, 222 Gray's Inn Road
London WC1X 8HB

Simon & Schuster: Celebrating 100 Years of Publishing in 2024

www.simonandschuster.co.uk
www.simonandschuster.com.au
www.simonandschuster.co.in

Simon & Schuster Australia, Sydney
Simon & Schuster India, New Delhi

A CIP catalogue record for this book
is available from the British Library.

PB ISBN 978-1-3985-1467-6
eBook ISBN 978-1-3985-1468-3
eAudio ISBN 978-1-3985-1469-0

Printed and Bound in the UK using 100%
Renewable Electricity at CPI Group (UK) Ltd

MIX
Paper | Supporting
responsible forestry
FSC
www.fsc.org
FSC® C171272

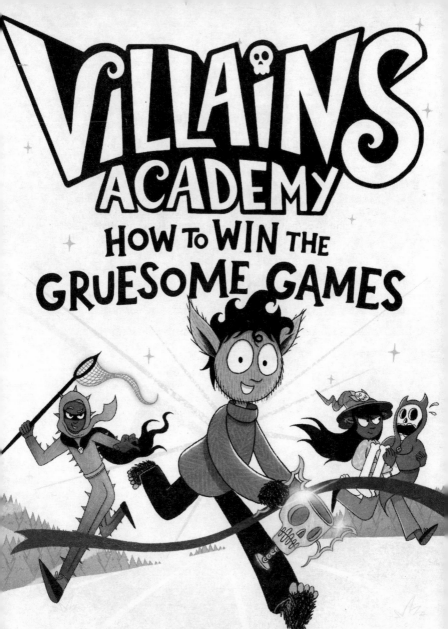

VILLAINS ACADEMY

HOW TO WIN THE GRUESOME GAMES

Written, illustrated and designed by

RYAN HAMMOND

SIMON AND SCHUSTER

GRUESOME GAMES

For Mitch. My partner in crime.
The Mona to my Bram. The Sheila
to her cake. Thank you for everything x

ABOUT TO EXPLODE

The Cereal Killers sat in the food hall of Villains Academy playing a game of exploding snap. Bram the werewolf shovelled a grilled cheese and bad-bean sandwich into his mouth, while trying to decide on his next move.

Sheila the ghost peeked at Bryan the lion's cards while he napped and Skele-tony, who was better known as just Tony, kept his cards close to his chest and threatened to take his own arm off and whack anyone who came near him. Only Mona the elf witch kept her cards face up on the table without a care in the world. Nobody dared mess with Mona or they'd be zapped into next year by her magical net.

'Who do you think would win a fight out of Master Mardybum and Guru Gertrude?' Bram asked as he played his next card and grimaced, waiting for an explosion. But none came – *phew*!

'That's easy,' Sheila the ghost said with a flick of her tail. 'Guru Gertrude.'

'Are you out of your mind? No *way* would Guru Gertrude win against Mardybum!' Tony exclaimed as he slammed down a card on top of Bram's. 'Gertrude has no magic powers, apart from badly predicting the future.'

'Don't be so rude, bony Tony,' Sheila said. 'Having powers doesn't necessarily mean you'll win.'

'Most of the winners of the Gruesome Games over the years had powers,' said Mona. 'And even better, the games have *no rules*. Cheating, underhand tactics and foul play are advised and encouraged. You can do whatever you need to do to win, without worrying about getting *any* detentions!' she concluded as she confidently placed down her card on the pile in the centre of the table and was met by a blinding flash and deafening

BANG!

'HA! I win!' Tony shouted as he threw out his arms and collected the winning cards for himself.

Sheila smirked at Mona. 'I thought your powers gave you an edge, sonny peep?'

The elf witch frowned like a sore loser. 'Not in exploding snap. But they will definitely help in the Gruesome Games tomorrow. That Trouble Trophy will be ours!'

Bram swallowed the last bite of his sandwich and tried not to think about the embarrassment he was doomed to experience tomorrow. The games, which were basically a sports day for villains, had been weighing on his mind for the last month and the thought of having to lose in front of the entire year group and their parents made him feel sick. 'About the games tomorrow . . . I don't think I'm feeling too well,' Bram said and rubbed his belly dramatically.

'Excuse me, we'll have less of the fake illness,' Sheila said as she zoomed up to Bram's face. 'We have to play as a team tomorrow and if you aren't with us, then we don't have a team. Now, you're not going to want to crush my dreams, are you, Bram?' Sheila put on her best puppy eyes.

Bram sighed. He had been paired up with the Cereal Killers on his first day at Villains Academy, and now they had become his allies and best friends. 'I'm not quite at the dream-crushing level of villain yet, I suppose.'

'Fantabulous!' Sheila replied.

'You're not still worried about your parents coming, are you?' Tony asked as he packed away the box of exploding snap.

'PARENTS?!'

Bryan jerked awake.

'Where?'

'Behind you!' Sheila joked, making the lion jump in fright.

Mona laughed. 'Don't worry, they're not here until tomorrow.'

'Phew,' Bryan sighed. 'I'm glad it's only for the day. Parents are so annoying, aren't they? It'll be nice for them to watch us win the Gruesome Games, though.'

A loud laugh came from behind them, which made Bryan jump even higher this time. Behind him stood their nemeses, the Overlords, with evil expressions on their faces. Mal, a Frankenstein-esque boy, stood in the centre as if he was in charge. Close behind was the Tooth Hairy, with her long hair that could wrap around her enemies and crush them. Mr Toad stood licking his lips menacingly, while Jeeves the cat and Spike the crocodile sneered at the Cereal Killers.

'You think you're going to win the
Gruesome Games tomorrow?' Mal jibed.
'Don't be ridiculous! You couldn't win
them in a million years. Not with Bram
on your team, anyway.'

The Overlords laughed. Bram crossed
his arms and ignored them. He wouldn't
rise to their childish taunting – he was

used to it by now, having been at Villains
Academy for almost a year.

'And yet not one of you has a single
evil talent,' Mona said, rising from
her seat. 'If any of you come near us
tomorrow, I'll trap you in my net and
fling you deep into the Wicked Woods
where nobody will ever find you.'

'We'll see about that.' The Tooth Hairy shrugged as the gang walked away with wicked smiles on their faces. It was only Mal who turned round as he exited the main doors and dragged the side of his hand across his neck as he stared at Bram. *Dead meat*, he mouthed.

'Ignore him,' Sheila said, blocking Bram's view. 'He's only doing it because he fancies you.'

Tony spat out his drink across the table, which splattered Bryan in the face. 'Sheila, what are you talking about?' Tony laughed.

'I read in a book that people are only mean to you because they fancy you. They're trying to get your attention,' Sheila replied matter-of-factly.

'And it's nothing to do with the fact that we're at a school for villains, so people are just mean all the time?' Mona smirked.

'Not at all,' Sheila said.

'Okay . . .' Bram replied and quickly tried to change the subject before his fur grew even hotter. 'So, who else's parents are coming tomorrow?'

'My grandma is coming,' Mona said. 'It's so annoying that they make everyone's parents come to watch. Nobody wants their parents here.'

Bram nodded his head. It was going to be a difficult day. But he was glad that Mona's grandma was coming, because her parents were always too busy to make time for her. And Bram couldn't wait to introduce her to his dads. Since starting at the school she had become one of his best friends . . . possibly his *bestest* friend. But he couldn't say that out loud without the rest of the Cereal Killers getting upset. 'I'm looking forward to introducing you to my dads. They've heard a lot about you. All bad, of course,' Bram added.

'I should hope so.' Mona frowned. 'What about you, Tony?'

Tony shuffled uncomfortably in his chair. 'Yeah, my dad is coming.'

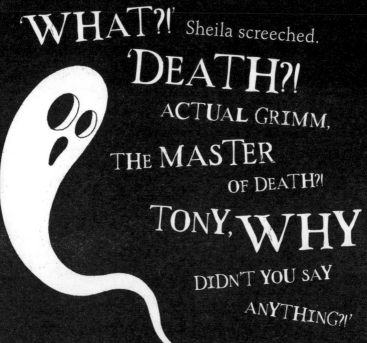

'WHAT?!' Sheila screeched. 'DEATH?! ACTUAL GRIMM, THE MASTER OF DEATH?! TONY, WHY DIDN'T YOU SAY ANYTHING?!'

'Because I didn't want you to react like that!' Tony said and poked his pinkie through Sheila's head to calm her down. 'He's just my dad.'

'Just your dad *and* the master of death,' Sheila swooned. 'You're going to put all *our* parents to shame! See, Bram, you have nothing to worry about. Tony is chill about his dad coming, so you should be chill about yours too. Oh, my, what a day tomorrow is going to be!'

Bram nodded to shut Sheila up, but it wasn't that easy to calm his mind. He had always felt that he had something to prove with his dads and they always expected so much from him. Plus, it didn't help that his Papa Percevil had won the Gruesome Games with his teammates when he was at Villains Academy. Whereas Bram wasn't naturally evil and had needed to work hard to get his place at the school. He wanted to make his parents proud, but everything he did seemed to go wrong and lead to embarrassment. He didn't understand how *not* to care about what other people thought about him. But with all the first years, their parents *and* teachers watching the Gruesome Games . . . that much pressure could make him mess everything up. He didn't want to be the disappointment of the family. He wanted to carry on the family line and win the Gruesome Games for them, just like his dad wanted. But that seemed impossible.

As his friends chatted away about Tony's dad and the bell rang to mark the end of lunch, Bram began to think of excuses that would get him out of

competing in the Gruesome Games . . .
and at this point death seemed like a
very good option.

CHAPTER 2

THE FOUNDERS OF VILLAINS ACADEMY

Bram fought the urge to close his eyes and go to sleep as his History of Evil teacher droned on about matters of the past. But just as he was drifting off to sleep, something Chief Crabbatus said caught his attention.

'One hundred years ago, five friends banded together to found Villains Academy,' the teacher said as he blew dust off the pages of his book.

'The founders, as they are known, all shared a love of pranks, badness and evil deeds. They enjoyed spreading evil through the world and Villains Academy became an immediate success. The founders created the Gruesome Games along with the school to test the talents of fledgling first-year villains – and to have a bit of fun. They will be the ones hosting the games tomorrow, so remember to be respectful.'

Bram sat up straight and grabbed his pen for the first time in almost an hour, ready to take notes. Usually he wouldn't be so bothered, but he wanted to find out as much as he could about the famous founders before the games tomorrow. He needed all the help he could get.

'The most famous founder, which is highly contested between the five friends, is Sir Nevil. Pronounced, "knee-vil" like evil. Quite easy to remember,' the teacher continued.

'Nevil the weasel,' Sheila whispered across the table to the other Cereal Killers.

'Nevil the weasel painting on an easel,' Tony the skeleton replied.

Chief Crabbatus let out a huff and launched his dusty book across the room at Tony. It knocked his head off his shoulders and sent it flying through the air. This wasn't unusual for the teacher, who went through at least forty books in a lesson, launching them at his students to shut them up.

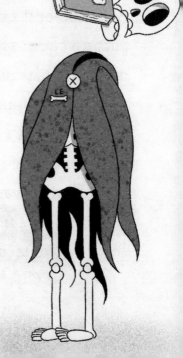

'The founders met while they were at school. A normal school.' The teacher shuddered, then continued, 'They were the naughtiest students in their year group. They got to know each other in detention, where they spent most of their time. At first, they began as enemies, outdoing each other on who could carry out the most elaborate prank and be the meanest, most horrible child in the school. But by the time they left, they were the best of friends and on the same path to cause as much destruction and mayhem as possible.'

'I like the sound of them,' Bram said to Mona with a smile, before ducking below his desk as a book flew towards his head.

Beside him, Sheila had collected Tony's skull and was attempting to screw it back on to his body.

'Stop chitchatting and listen,' the teacher warned. 'Twice a year the founders of Villains Academy rise from their graves on the grounds to visit the school – once for the Gruesome Games and once for graduation. Tomorrow will be one of the biggest days of your lives, so don't mess it up.'

Bram gulped as pressure built up in his chest. 'Could you give us any tips on how to win the games, chief?' he asked.

'No.' Chief Crabbatus frowned. 'The games were set up by the founders for first years to prove their perilous pranking skills. There will be three games spread throughout the day. They will all be team games: one will take

place indoors, one will involve your teachers and the final one will be a surprise extravaganza of pure evilness. The games get harder with each round, but that final Gruesome Game will be brutal. The aim is to deceive your way through the games and destroy your enemies as you go. The overall winning team will receive the Trouble Trophy and secure their names in the famous *Book of Bad* – a yearbook of all the *worst* students to attend Villains Academy. And this year marks one hundred years of the games, so I'm sure there'll be a few surprises in store. Tomorrow could change your entire career as a villain. No pressure.'

Bram took a deep breath and attempted to control the worries that were swirling around in his head. He knew that he was a talented villain, but he didn't know if he would be bad enough to get his name in the *Book of Bad* when there were so many fledgling villains to compete with, even though it was something that he had dreamed about since before coming to Villains Academy.

And it didn't help Bram's nerves that the Overlords were making threats from across the room. The Tooth Hairy pretended to choke Mr Toad with strands of hair, predicting the fate of whoever crossed her in the games. Mal dragged his finger across his neck and mimed his head falling off. Jeeves released his claws and tore through the sheets of homework that Chief Crabbatus handed out, while pointing threateningly at Mona. And Spike snapped his jaws, pretending to chew up his enemies.

But the Cereal Killers gave back as

good as they got. Tony cracked his knuckles. Sheila threatened to fly through the Overlords' heads and give them brain freeze. Mona pretended to zap them all with their net, while Bryan mimed squashing them with his big paws. Bram pulled faces back and spent most of his time watching the clock as the minutes ticked by and the Gruesome Games drew closer.

When the bell rang at the end of the lesson, Bram could only hope that the next and final lesson of the day would help draw out his courage.

CHAPTER 3

INVISIBLE (ST)INK

Master Mardybum stood in the greenhouse with a face like a slapped bottom as Class Z entered for their Poison lesson. 'Chop chop! Some of us haven't got all day,' he grumbled.

The Cereal Killers took their usual seats on a table far away from the Overlords as Master Mardybum began writing instructions on the blackboard. Bram had a love-hate relationship with

Master Mardybum. In his first week, his tutor had underestimated him and thought him weak. But Bram proved him wrong by winning the Mystery Maze – a series of tasks set by the teacher to prove their badness. Then Bram proved him wrong again in his second term by taking down his ex-teacher, Felix Frostbite, when he tried to steal all the dragons from the Wicked Woods. Now, they weren't exactly the best of friends, but Bram felt like Master Mardybum was starting to respect him as a villain.

'Today we will be learning how to make an invisible-ink poison,' Master Mardybum said.

The class looked at each other in bewilderment.

'There's more to invisible ink than writing down your sad little secrets in your diaries,' Master Mardybum began, with a swoosh of his enormous sleeves. 'Invisible ink can be used to record powerful spells, particularly protective enchantments. If you write those in invisible ink around your doorway, there's no way an enemy can enter. It can make a strong defensive barrier and you can even cover yourself in it to turn invisible. Though you'd need a lot of it and the illusion would only last ten minutes. After that the unicorn gloop in the poison reacts with your body heat and turns into a bogey-like consistency on your skin.'

Bram wrinkled his nose and beside him, Bryan licked his lips.

'You could also use invisible ink to cheat in your exams . . .' the teacher continued, at which all of the students' ears pricked up. 'But you'll not get away with that at Villains Academy. The bookworm's special eyesight can see invisible ink from a mile away. So don't even bother trying if you value your life.'

'Ugh! Not fair,' Sheila complained. 'What happens if you drink it? Will it turn you invisible?'

Master Mardybum grinned. 'It's a poison, so I wouldn't drink it if I were you. It wouldn't kill you, but it would give you a terrible bellyache that would make you explode from the inside out.'

'Wow, really?' Tony's eyes bulged.

'No,' Mona rolled her eyes. 'He means you'll have the farts and will end up like Bryan.'

'Exactly,' Mardybum agreed.

'Hey!' Bryan protested. 'I don't fart that much.'

'*Yes, you do!*' the Cereal Killers all said in unison.

'Invisible ink is a quick poison to prepare and can be made in less than twenty-four hours. But it does include some of the rarest ingredients known to villains – so I want no spillages or accidents or I'm going to come and personally steal your pocket money to pay for them, okay?!' Master Mardybum gave Bram his famous death stare. 'This right here is unicorn gloop. Do you know what part of the unicorn its gloop comes from?'

'Its bum,' said Sheila, which Master Mardybum conveniently ignored.

'Its tears!' Mr Toad shouted.

'Good guess, but no,' the teacher replied. 'Those are much rarer and more expensive than its gloop. Anyone else?'

'Its saliva,' Mona said with a hint of boredom. 'It comes from a unicorn's saliva.'

'Correct once again, Little Miss Know-it-all,' Master Mardybum praised. Mona rolled her eyes.

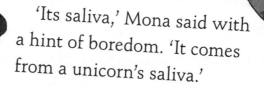

'Unicorn gloop, or unicorn drool, has sparkling qualities and is a key ingredient in invisible ink. Combine it with the tears of ghosts . . .'

Sheila gasped.

' . . . and a few stems of a starwart plant to create a paste,' Mardybum said. 'The paste needs to be stretched and tossed until it bounces off the floor like a rubber ball. Once it's thick and springy, you can let it rest overnight where it will turn into a shimmering liquid. If you make it correctly, I'll let you keep it . . . to do with as you wish.'

The Cereal Killers grinned at each other. Bram began to think about everything he could do with his ink – starting with putting a protective enchantment around his bed so that Sheila would stop tickling his toes.

'The instructions are on the blackboard, and *please* don't disturb me. I have a complex knitting pattern that I'd like to finish today.' Master Mardybum lounged back in his chair and began stabbing his knitting needles together threateningly, daring anyone to disturb him.

Bram and the Cereal Killers poured the ingredients out on to the desk and began making their pastes. 'Ew.' Sheila

grimaced. 'This smells *exactly* like your morning breath, Tony.'

Tony raised his head and tried to grab his own arm to whack Sheila with, but found himself stuck together by the sticky gloop.

'You're going to want to work quickly, otherwise the ingredients will turn too bogey-like,' Mona said as she kneaded her paste masterfully. 'And it's the

unicorn gloop that smells like morning breath. What did you expect? It comes from their mouths.' Bram stood next to Mona, copying her movements as he kneaded his paste. He had always admired Mona's skill with poisons and this was one that he definitely wanted to get right if he was going to keep it. 'Are you looking forward to seeing your grandma tomorrow?' Bram asked.

'Yes,' Mona said, not taking her eyes off her work. She hated talking about anything personal, especially her feelings, but over the past few months Bram had been working on getting her to open up to him. 'It'll be nice,' she added, noticing Bram's stare. 'I haven't seen her in ages and it'll be good for her to see how far I've come as a villain. I'm not sure if she'll like you, though . . .'

'Why not?!' Bram exclaimed, trying not to feel offended.

'She doesn't like werewolves.'

Bram opened his mouth to argue back when he noticed Mona was laughing. 'That's not funny,' Bram said with a smile. 'You know I'm nervous about tomorrow. I don't need to worry about your grandma hating me too!'

'Oh, chill your beans. It'll be fine. By this time tomorrow, our names will be in the *Book of Bad* and you'll be wondering what you were worried about,' Mona said as she began tossing the dough-like paste around her head like a pizza.

'Show-off,' Bryan moaned. He'd already given up on his poison.

'Wow!' Sheila gasped. 'I want to try that!'

'I don't think you shoul—' Bram began, but it was too late. Sheila began whipping her paste around like a rope, which stretched longer every time she twirled. It sent nearby vials flying and almost took out Mr Toad, who was busy trying to see if his own paste had started bouncing yet.

'My turn, my turn!' Tony joined in. He spun the paste around in his hand and shouted 'MAMMA MIA!' at the top of his lungs.

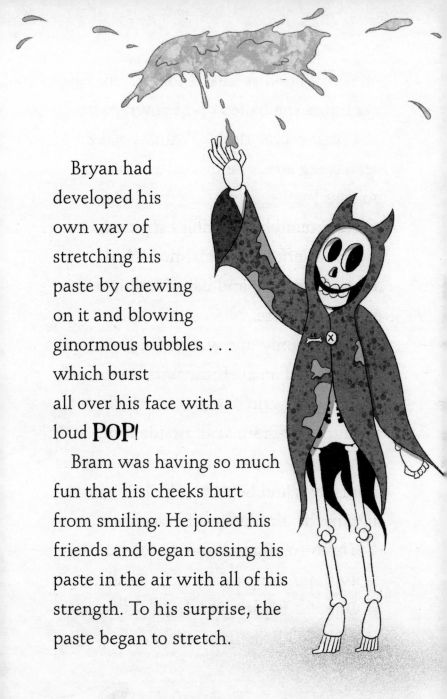

Bryan had
developed his
own way of
stretching his
paste by chewing
on it and blowing
ginormous bubbles . . .
which burst
all over his face with a
loud **POP**!

Bram was having so much
fun that his cheeks hurt
from smiling. He joined his
friends and began tossing his
paste in the air with all of his
strength. To his surprise, the
paste began to stretch.

'You're good at this!' Mona said with a smile as she balled up her own paste and sat it on the desk. 'I think you've been lying about being bad at making poisons.'

'No, I really am terrible. This one is just easier than most. I think I'm done,' Bram said and balled up his own poisonous paste.

'There's only one way to find out.' Mona raised an eyebrow with a wickedly mischievous grin.

'In three?' Bram said. Beside him, Bryan, Tony and Sheila all readied themselves and held their blobs of paste high in the air like deadly weapons.

'Three . . .' Bram began.

'Two . . .' Tony said.

'One . . .' Bryan roared.

'BOUNCE!' Sheila screeched.

The gang launched their pastes to the floor. Tony's splattered like a pancake. Bryan's bounced back into his face and almost gave him a black eye. Sheila's stuck to her tail and sent her flying through the air and Mona's bounced perfectly back into her hand.

Meanwhile, Bram's bounced with such force against the floor that it soared through the classroom and right into Master Mardybum's lap, making him topple backwards off his chair.

'Who threw this?!' the teacher shouted as he gathered himself off the ground and held up Bram's paste with menace in his eyes.

Fear crept from Bram's toes right up to the top of his head as he fought not to throw up. 'It was me, sir,' Bram said bravely. Once upon a time, Bram would have cowered away and not owned up to his actions for fear of being shouted at or destroyed. But he was a villain now, and he was proud of the poison that he had created . . . and the mess he had made of Master Mardybum's knitting.

Then his teacher did something that scared Bram even more than shouting. His mouth twitched with the faintest smile. 'Not a bad job.' Master Mardybum nodded. 'This looks like a perfect paste. By this time tomorrow, you should have a vial of invisible ink. Well done.'

Bram smiled and felt a surge of pride swell in his chest. He took back his paste without saying thank you . . . because there was nothing Master Mardybum hated more than good manners.

For the rest of the lesson, the students filled in worksheets and learnt about the ingredients of invisible ink and where they came from, along with other creative ways to use it. Bram let his mind wander to the Gruesome Games and tried not to dream about how by this time tomorrow his life as a villain could have changed forever. He'd just made a perfect poison, something that he had never achieved before, and if that didn't prove how far he had come as a villain, then he didn't know what did. Maybe he and his friends could win the Gruesome Games after all.

As the bell rang to mark the end of the school day, Bram walked out of the greenhouse with a skip in his step. But

as they left, Master Mardybum uttered a
warning to the students. 'I'll see all of you
on the front lawn tomorrow morning at
six a.m. And *don't* be late. The founders
will not be as lenient as I am . . .'

CHAPTER 4

THE BOOK OF BAD

Bram spent the majority of his evening worrying, so he decided to take a late-night trip to the library to distract himself. His friends were happy to tag along.

The library was one of Bram's favourite places in the school and at this time of day it was blissfully quiet. Ornate iron lanterns hung between the aisles of books and moonflies hovered around them, lighting up the air like

magical fairies protecting their land.
Moonflies provide the best reading light,
without damaging any of the wood
in the paper. Flecks of dust floated in
the rays as Bram browsed the shelves,
running his fingers along the spines of
the books.

Some books were chunky, while
others were thin. Some had foiled details
all over them whereas others were plain.
They were all different and told different
stories – just like people. Bram thought
that if he was a book, he'd probably be a
normal-sized one. Not too thin and not
too thick. Maybe with a knitted ribbon
and cosy jacket to keep him warm. The
thought made him smile.

Tony enjoyed the library late at night
because he liked to listen to the sound
of his bones clicking down the quiet

bookshelves. Bryan said that the library was his favourite place to nap and Sheila was always up for an adventure. Mona, like Bram, was happy to spend some time reading and learning new things.

'Are you sure we can't go and get some cake?' Sheila asked.

'No!' they all replied in unison. Sheila's trips to the kitchen always ended in disaster.

At the far end of the shelves, under a huge portrait of the five founders, stood a lone circular table which had been carved into by the past students of Villains Academy. Bram started to read the names of students who had scratched and forced their names into the wood, but it wasn't the table that caught his attention. It was the book that was lying atop it.

The Book of Bad.

The legendary yearbook of the
worst students who'd ever attended
Villains Academy. It sat on a stand in
the middle of the table, a lamp above
illuminating its pages and the names
within. Its leather-bound cover was soft
and decorated with detailed stitching.
Patterns of dragons, shields and the
Villains Academy logo covered the

surface. It glowed with magic, and Bram was pretty sure that it *was* magic. The book had been made by the founders after all, and if they could rise from the graves of the school, then a magical book was quite ordinary by comparison.

'Ah. Admiring the *Book of Bad* again, Bram? That's the third time this week,' a voice behind Bram spoke, making him jump. The chief librarian, Helen Wordsmith the Third, stared at him with a warm smile.

Bram smiled back and picked up the *Book of Bad* as he had done many times before. It buzzed in his hands and a thin, glowing chain locked it to the table to stop him from stealing or destroying it. Bram flicked through the pages, reading about past villains and their evil achievements in winning the Gruesome

Games. Most had won for performing exceptionally well in famous games such as the Head-and-Spoon Race and defeating a creature called the three-legged lurgy while hula-hooping a ring of fire.

But Bram wasn't bothered about most of the past villains of Villains Academy. He flicked the pages to the one name that he did care about: *Percevil Moon*. His dad's name sat on the page as part of history, documenting his win at the Gruesome Games for the quickest *ever* one-hundred-metre sprint through the Wicked Woods. Seeing his dad's name made Bram smile, but it also filled him with dread. He was never going to live up to his fathers' legacy or their dream of him winning the games.

He put the book back on the table with a definite THUD.

'Ah, the book has a way of doing that. How can you ever live up to the villains of yesterday? Try not to dwell on them, and focus on yourself. Here,' Helen said, passing Bram a quill. 'You should add your name to it.'

'What?!' Bram protested in shock. 'I can't do that! That's cheating.'

'Chicken.' Helen shrugged.

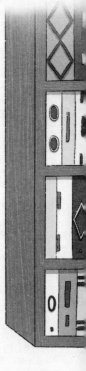

'I'm not a chicken,' Bram replied, his fur growing hot with embarrassment.

'Then do it, *chicken*.'

'No!' Bram said, growing angrier. 'Aren't you the chief librarian? You shouldn't be encouraging me to scribble in your books.'

Helen ignored Bram and began wiggling her arms and spinning in a circle. 'Cluck, cluck, cluck, cluck . . .'

'Oh, Helen's doing her legendary chicken impression,' Sheila said, appearing behind her. 'I love it when she does this! Cluck, cluck, cluck, cluck . . .'

'I'm NOT a chicken,' Bram shouted. In a huff, he grabbed the quill out of the librarian's hand and whipped open the *Book of Bad* to a blank page. Bram pressed the quill into the paper and began scribbling his name.

But no ink transferred on to the page and before Bram could acknowledge what was happening, a loud ZAP buzzed through his body and sent him flying off his feet.

'I forgot to say . . .' Helen laughed. 'Only the founders can write in the *Book of Bad*. Think of how many people would sneak their name in if not!'

Bram pushed himself off the floor and attempted to flatten his frazzled fur. 'A warning would have been nice. Why did you egg me on like that?'

'Sozzle.' Helen shrugged. 'I haven't seen anyone be zapped in *ages* and it gives me such a thrill. Sir Nevil would love to see you right now with your hair like that. He loves a prank – he's the King of Pranks! He was the one who started the whole pranking war with the rest of the founders when he was at school with them. There's a whole book on the pranks he's pulled: from hiding under students' beds to terrify them, to filling people's shoes with spiders and even fooling everyone with fake exam results. One year, the whole school thought they'd failed! I think there's only one prank he never managed to pull off.'

'What prank was that?' Tony asked, appearing from behind a pile of books with the rest of the Cereal Killers.

'Hmm, where's that book?' Helen pondered and stretched out her arm. In an instant, a book flew through the air and landed softly in her palm.

'Here it is! The only prank that Sir Nevil never managed to pull off, much to his embarrassment, was a simple classic. He attempted to draw moustaches on his friends while they slept, but came up short when he was caught by his fellow founder Zyla, who proceeded to get her revenge by replacing his shampoo with hair-removal cream . . . making him lose all of his hair AND his precious moustache. History reports that it took him three years to grow it back.'

'Brutal,' Mona said. 'I love it.'

'Yes,' Helen agreed with a wicked smile. 'Now, you villains should be off to bed because it's a big day for us all tomorrow. Here, take some books and off you pop.'

The chief librarian filled the arms of the Cereal Killers with books and ushered them out of the library towards their dormitory.

Bram stayed up reading facts about the founders and the pranks they played long after everyone else had gone to sleep. He snuck under the covers and read late into the night . . . eventually falling asleep with a newfound determination to prove himself, take down the Overlords and maybe even pull off the prank of a lifetime.

CHAPTER 5

THE RETURN OF EVIL

Bram wiped sleep from his eyes as he sat on the grass in front of Villains Academy with the rest of the Cereal Killers. A thick morning mist hung close to the ground and Bram tried to ignore the wet dew that seeped through his trousers and the heavy feeling of pressure that weighed on his shoulders.

Dotted around the lawn were the rest of the first-year classes. They were all waiting expectantly for the legendary founders to ascend from their graves. All eyes were pinned on the ornate gates of the graveyard, waiting for their arrival.

Vines grew around them and moss clung to the brickwork. The place had an ominous feeling about it – it was definitely somewhere you wanted to avoid. No students were permitted to enter. Rumour said that if you dared put one foot through the gates, evil spirits would rise from the graves and banish you. There were also rumours about child-eating monsters, humongous spiders and devilish vines coming after you. Bram was quite happy staying in the comfort of Villains Academy.

'Straighten your shirt!' Master Mardybum roared at a student to the gang's left, before making his way over to

them. 'Bram. Have you brushed your hair today? You look like you've been plugged into a socket. Sort it out, will you?!'

'It's because of that stupid book last night,' Bram complained to his friends, while trying to pat down his fur.

'SIR!' Guru Gertrude shouted across the lawn and waved her arms like she had ants in her pants. 'Look! The sun. It's rising.'

Behind the Wicked Woods to the left, the sun peeked over the horizon to say hello.

'**POSITIONS, EVERYONE!**' Master Mardybum screamed. He ran over to join the teachers and greet their guests by the

gates to the forbidden graveyard.

Rays of sunshine speckled the grass, making the morning dew shine like sprinkled diamonds. A light breeze began to blow and with an enormous **CRACK** the mist of the graveyard began to swirl. Bram held his breath. Sheila floated still for the first time in her life (and death). Mona smiled wickedly. Bryan's eyes almost popped out of his head and Tony shook with anticipation.

One by one, the legendary founders emerged from their graves. Bram felt time stop and tried to take in the moment – he was never going to witness this again.

Sir Nevil

The first founder to emerge was Sir Nevil. His long black cloak billowed behind him as he floated towards the teachers to greet them. His body was long and green, and a twirly moustache sat high up on his face, drawing attention to his furrowed brows and the look of menace glistening in his eyes.

The only thing that Bram thought looked friendly about him was his chunky turtleneck jumper.

The second founder to arrive was Zyla, a fierce-looking woman with a terrifying net and a resting grumpy-face that could put

Zyla

Master Mardybum's death stare to the test. She was shortly followed by Master Masonnaise, a deadly sandwich known for slapping people around the face. He wore a wicked smile and moved so fast Bram couldn't keep track of him.

Then came Ser Bona Lisa, a famous warrior and fighter in the form of a skeleton. Her armour glinted in the morning rays, almost blinding the students. And finally, the last founder, Lord Moon Moon, trotted up through the mist. He moved gracefully for a giant wolf,

Ser Bona Lisa

Lord Moon Moon

but his eyes narrowed suspiciously at his surroundings. Lord Moon Moon's ears twitched as if they could hear sounds from miles away and he walked with his chest puffed out, right into Ser Bona Lisa, who tumbled and went skittering across the lawn.

'Damn it, Moon Moon,' Ser Bona Lisa hissed as she pulled herself back together. 'Watch what you're doing. Just because you've been asleep for half a year doesn't mean you can just walk into me.'

'Son of a monkey, don't start with me so early. Maybe *you* should watch where *you're* going,' Lord Moon Moon replied.

'I thought they might look old and crusty,' Sheila whispered to her friends. 'What with them being underground for many months of the year.'

Tony shook his head. 'Sheila, as a

ghost, you of all people should know better. Are you old and crusty?'

Bram laughed. 'Is it just me, or are they sort of . . . glowing?'

'They're immortal,' Mona said. 'They're the top level of badness you can ever reach.'

Master Mardybum hurried around the founders, doing a mixture of curtseying, bowing and hand-shaking. As he took Sir Nevil's hand, Master Mardybum screeched with surprise. Sir Nevil burst into laughter and showed off a shocking device in his palm, at which the other founders sniggered.

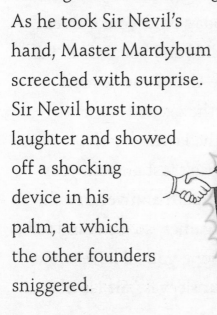

Pranksters, Bram thought with a smile. It was nice to see Mardybum get a taste of his own medicine for a change.

Master Mardybum muttered quietly and hurried back to his fellow teachers as the blood rose to his cheeks, making him glow a luscious shade of magenta.

'VILLAINS,' Sir Nevil announced with a fierce glare. 'Thank you for gathering here for our arrival. We are most honoured. For today and today only, your classes have been cancelled and you will all be competing in the Gruesome Games!'

A cheer from the excited students echoed around the lawn.

'But this year isn't just any old year . . . it's the one-hundredth anniversary since we founded the games, so it's going to be a special one. I hope you all have some *evil* tricks up your sleeves,' Sir Nevil said.

Zyla walked forward with her arms crossed, followed by the other three founders. They stood beside Sir Nevil in a line like a pop band.

'The rules are simple,' Zyla began.

'THERE ARE NO RULES.'

Mutterings whispered around the grass and Sheila wiggled in excitement. Bram attempted to control the anxiety rising in his chest. He was terrified of failure and going down in history as an embarrassment – and on the one-hundredth anniversary of the games, too! Everyone would remember that.

'There will be three games set over the course of the day,' Master Masonnaise said. 'The overall winning team will win the coveted Trouble Trophy and their names will be entered in the *Book of Bad*. The final decision will be ours. We won't necessarily choose the team that won the most games, but the one whose evilness has impressed us the most. Our decision is final.'

'Agreed.' Ser Bona Lisa scowled.

Lord Moon Moon grinned, showing razor-sharp teeth. 'Your parents and guardians will be arriving soon. Let's go and greet them.'

Bram steadied his nerves and took courage from his friends as they walked towards the entrance of Villains Academy to greet their parents. The sun was rising higher over the trees and the grounds were eerily quiet as the founders placed their hands on their hips with wicked grins. The air began to rumble and loud wings thundered across the

skies. Like meteors crashing to earth, skull-shaped carriages pulled by young dragons landed on the lawn by the entrance to Villains Academy. Silence filled the air and was broken by the creaking of carriage doors as the parents and guardians stepped out on to the lawn.

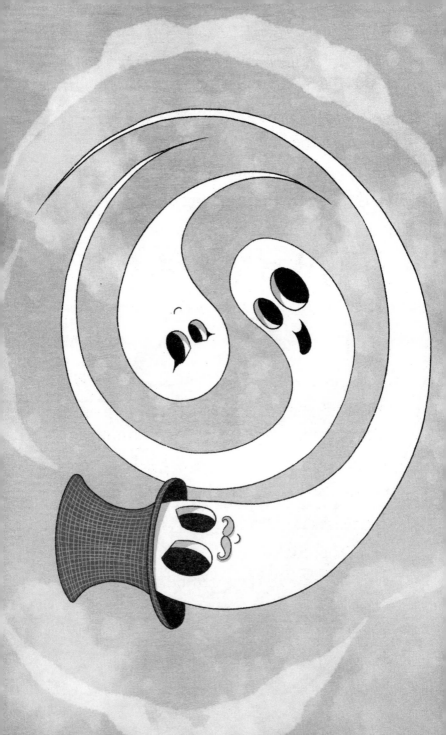

CHAPTER 6

GRUESOME GAME ONE: SNACK RACE

Fledgling villains welcomed their parents and guardians as they arrived. Some students rushed towards their families and gave them hugs. Others did fist bumps and complicated handshakes. Some didn't hug at all and frowned at each other like worst enemies.

Sheila twirled through the air with her parents, who screeched with joy even louder than she did. Bryan bounded

towards his mum and dad and then all
three of them proceeded to play-fight
and roll around on the grass, growling
loudly. Mona greeted her grandma with
an eye-roll while Tony gave a very
respectful nod to his father, who in turn
bowed his head as he gripped his scythe.
He was fascinated by the way all the
families were so
different.

'Let's see how
much you've
learnt at this
school,' Tony's
dad said to
him. 'If you
win the
Gruesome

Games, I'll consider letting you stay.'

Bram flinched and looked away, not wanting to eavesdrop. But what did 'letting you stay' mean? His thoughts were quickly distracted as his dads walked towards him. 'Hi, Dad. Hi, Papa,' he said as he squished them into a hug. They smelled of smoke and freshly cut grass and their lambswool jumpers scratched against his fur.

'It's good to see you, Bram.' Papa Percevil smiled and ruffled his hair. 'You look like you've grown.'

'Yes, you look like you're getting big and strong,' Dad Derek replied, squeezing Bram against his side, making him shriek.

'Stop it,' Bram said, pushing them off. 'You're embarrassing me. I'm a villain now! I need to look strong in front of my peers.'

'Oh, I know you are! And today you're going to prove that,' his dad said with a grin.

Bram averted his eyes and attempted to ignore the weight of family honour pressing down on his mind. 'Come on,' he said, changing the subject. 'I want you to meet my friends.'

The Cereal Killers were gathered nearby and one by one they all said hello and introduced each other to their parents. Bryan's parents almost snapped Bram's paws off when he offered a handshake. Tony's dad, the master of death, did nothing but nod and stare into Bram's soul. Sheila's parents zoomed through his head and gave him the worst brain freeze he had ever had. Mona's grandma squinted and looked him up and down with disgust when he smiled at her.

Bram's dads, however, were delighted to meet each and every one of the gang and pulled them all into squishy hugs . . . much to Mona's displeasure.

Cook and her band of cronies walked out of the main doors of the school with ladles and spatulas gripped tightly in their hands as weapons. 'Breakfast is served!' Cook bellowed over the noise, giving everyone a mean stare.

'Woohoo!' Sheila whooped.

'Oh, you don't think it's going to be that easy, do you?' Sir Nevil said as he grinned at the fledgling villains. 'To earn your breakfast, first you must fight for it. Let the Gruesome Games commence . . .'

The whole school had been set up for the Gruesome Games. The students were taken down to the kitchens in the basement where the first indoor game would begin, while their parents and guardians lined the corridors and stairways to watch the race.

There would be a rest for breakfast after the first game, followed by the second game involving the teachers. And then there would be lunch before the final and hardest Gruesome Game started in the afternoon. The day would be wrapped up with a midnight feast and an award ceremony to crown the winners of the Trouble Trophy.

'The first Gruesome Game will be a **SNACK RACE!**' Master Masonnaise declared. 'You must make your way through the kitchens, along the hallways and up the stairs to the food hall in your sacks. The first team to cross the line by the doors of the food hall with their sacks will be the winners. Anyone without their sack will lose the first game.'

'Oh, sonny peep, **I LOVE SNACKS!** My time has come!' Sheila squealed in excitement.

'He said sacks?' Tony frowned in confusion.

'No, he said sacks AND snacks!' Sheila replied giddily.

'Just make sure to keep hold of your sack,' Mona said with a hard glance at her friends. 'And watch each other's backs. We all need to cross the finish line to win.'

'Good plan,' Bram said.

'Remember, the rules are simple – there are no rules,' Zyla said.

'There will be obstacles along the way,' Ser Bona Lisa announced. 'It will be a true test of your physical ability . . . and will show how well you cope under pressure in a chaotic environment. Now, collect your sacks.'

The students pushed and shoved each other to get their sacks. The Cereal Killers fought their way to the front. Bram climbed between everyone's legs. Mona threatened people with her sizzling magical net. Sheila flew through

people's heads, while Tony rode on Bryan's back. 'Remember, stay together,' Mona whispered with a final, evil grin.

'May the best villains win,' Mal said beside them as the Overlords death-stared them out.

'Oh, trust me, we will,' Mona said

as she stepped into her sack with determination.

Mal laughed sarcastically. 'You're going down. The Cereal Killers have had far too much glory recently.'

'Bring it on,' Bram said, as determined as Mona.

The founders stood at the doors to the kitchen, their bodies glowing in the dim hallway as if they had eaten a hundred glowsticks each. They all opened their mouths and yelled in unison:

'BE BAD, NOT GOOD,

AND BRING YOUR EVIL OUT.

BE CUNNING AND WICKED,

BE READY WHEN WE SHOUT . . .

GO!'

Carnage erupted around Bram as the students stampeded into the kitchen. The Overlords yelled battle cries and hopped along in formation. Within seconds, Bram had lost sight of the Cereal Killers. He held on to his sack and jumped for his life as he and his fledgling villains bottlenecked in the doorway. Tony cried that he'd lost a finger while they tried to use Bryan as a battering ram to make way through the crowd. Sheila shocked anyone who came close, causing them to fall to the floor like sacks of potatoes, while Mona sizzled her enemies with her net, grabbing Bram by the arm to pull them back together.

'Stop moving!' Mona shouted to her friends as she halted, causing a pile-up behind her.

Bram stopped hopping and looked at

her in confusion. 'But we're meant to move forward! That's the whole aim of the game.'

Mona rolled her eyes. 'Bram, sometimes you really do fail to grasp being a villain. Just stand still.' Mona swung her net with her free hand and sizzled a hole in the bottom of Bram's sack. Then she did the same to the rest of the Cereal Killers' sacks . . . including all four on Bryan's paws.

Bram pushed his legs through the holes. 'Isn't this cheating?'

'There are no rules, Bram!' Mona shouted. Then a flying cake hit her in the face and she toppled to the ground. At the edges of the room, Cook and her cronies popped

up from behind pans
and utensils and began
launching all forms of
snacks towards the students. Now Bram
understood why the first game was called
a Snack Race. The snacks were there to
make the game harder.

Sheila shrieked in delight, catching
cakes in her mouth. A gigantic profiterole
zoomed into the centre of the
room and knocked over ten
students one by one
as if they were
bowling
pins.

Tony pulled off one arm and began using it like a bat, knocking aside cupcakes and cookies as if he were playing a game of cricket. Bryan bounded forward, using his size to his advantage, but came up short when he slipped on a vat of icing on the floor, causing him to tumble into a tower of plates that came crashing down with an almighty *SMASH*.

But the chaos created an opening as students hurled themselves out of the way of the flying plates – and the Cereal Killers took advantage. They burst through the gap and into the hallway where hundreds of watchful parents were gathered along the edges of the corridor and stairway. They cheered and screamed for

their children to win. Some parents
yelled insults at their children's
opponents, while others stuck
out a leg or two to trip
them up and slow
them down.

The Overlords were ahead, with the Cereal Killers hot on their heels. The holes in their sacks had given them an advantage, but now other fledgling villains copied their tactic so that they could run full-speed up the stairs.

Bram grabbed hold of the Tooth Hairy's leg and pulled her backwards into a group of terrified students. Mona dashed ahead of him and zapped Jeeves so that his fur stuck up at all angles – much to the delight of her grandmother who hollered from the side-lines. Sheila's parents screeched like banshees overhead, telling the Cereal Killers to get a move on.

Bram rushed up the stairs, dodging flying pastries, and focused on his end goal. The door to the food hall was just at the top of the stairs – and he was so close! All he had to do was get up the last few steps and make sure the Cereal Killers were with him. Then they would win.

But as his foot hit the final step, a hand latched around Bram's ankle, causing him to faceplant on the floor. Before Bram could stop him, Mal pulled Bram's sack off his legs and ran towards the finish line waving it like a flag. 'You can't win if you don't have a sack!' Mal shouted, and winked.

Bram kicked himself for not thinking of taking the sack off. He didn't have to wear it during the game, he just had to make sure he had it at the end!

The Cereal Killers gathered around him and pulled him to his feet. They yelled and spurred each other on while dodging flying bonbons and bananas. The gang skidded up to the main doors of the food hall. Tony used pan lids to defend them from flying cakes. Sheila used strawberry laces as ropes, ready to entangle everyone nearby.

But their efforts were no use as the Overlords approached the finish line. Bram felt a wave of evil wash over him as he watched Mal waving his sack in the air. In a final bid to stop them, Bram picked up a pancake, slathered in cream and maple syrup, off the floor and tossed it through the air like a boomerang. The pancake spun at speed and as Mal turned his head to see what the noise was, it hit him right in the face and slopped down his cheeks like a soggy face mask.

Mal toppled over the finish line and landed in a slump around his teammates. Screams of delight filled the air. The Cereal Killers crossed the line soon after, but the founders had already begun congratulating the Overlords on their win. They commended them on the tactic of stealing someone else's sack, and Sir Nevil shook his head at Bram.

Bram felt disappointed too. He wanted to play the Gruesome Games by the rules . . . but it turned out that there really were no rules. He hadn't thought that the founders actually meant it!

Everyone had to follow rules, right . . . ?
Though the essence of being a villain
was to break rules, so maybe Bram had
misunderstood the point in the first
place?

Bram tried to put on a brave face for his
friends and parents. Bryan cheered him up
by giving him a high-five for his incredible
pancake move. Mona smiled politely, but
muttered under her breath about revenge.
Sheila was busy licking cake and excess
food off everyone . . . while Tony stood in
silence, hanging his head.

'Are you okay, Tony?' Bram asked.

'No, I'm not. I can't lose you guys,'
Tony said sadly.

'It's okay, Tony,' Bram said and put his
arm around his friend. 'We're still here –
and we've only lost one game! We've got
two more games to prove ourselves, and

I think we were pretty badass, even if we didn't win.'

'No, you don't understand,' Tony said. 'If we don't win the Gruesome Games then my dad is going to take me out of Villains Academy.'

CHAPTER 7
FOUL PLAY

The Cereal Killers locked themselves
in the bathroom away from the
mischievous madness that had taken
over the school. Bram's heart was heavy
after learning that he might lose one of
his friends by the end of the day.

'And your dad won't change his mind?'
Mona asked.

'No,' Tony replied. 'He's stubborn. Once
he's decided you're going to die, there's no

changing his mind. And it's the same with this. Nobody argues with Death.'

'**WELL, SONNY PEEP,**' Sheila shouted. 'He's in for a shock because he's about to get his first-ever argument with ME. Where is he? I'll have a word.'

The Cereal Killers held back their laughter, but Tony shook his head. 'No, you'll just make it worse. We need to focus on performing well today, so he can see that I'm succeeding at Villains Academy. That this is the right path for my future.'

Bram sighed.

'Oh, big sigh,' Sheila said and patted Bram's head like a dog. 'What's wrong?'

'The games have become such a big deal,' Bram said. 'We're all trying to impress our families and achieve our own goals. I just feel like I can't breathe with the pressure.'

'I know how you feel,' Mona said as she sat next to Bram. 'I want to impress my grandma too. *And* I don't want to mess up my record for when we leave. Think of how good *Winner of the Gruesome Games* will look written on there!'

'We can't think like this,' Sheila said loudly over everyone. 'We always perform best when we work together, while having fun – and that was **SO MUCH FUN!** Let's just enjoy taking part. That way we'll win *and* hopefully get Tony's dad to change his mind.'

'You're right!' Bryan said as the gang gathered for a group hug.

'So, what's the plan?' Tony asked.

'Well, we don't know what the game is yet,' Mona said. 'But we need to take down the Overlords. They're our biggest competition right now.'

'And if we can impress the founders at the same time, that puts us in a good position to win,' Bram replied.

'Okay.' Tony smiled for the first time since the Snack Race. 'Take down the Overlords and impress the founders. We can do that.'

'**HELL, YES, WE CAN!**' Sheila screeched like a battle cry.

Bram threw his hand into the middle of his friends and smiled. 'In three . . . ?'

The gang placed their hands, paws, fingers and tails into the middle as Bram counted down, then they collectively shouted '**THE CEREAL KILLERS!**' at the top of their lungs.

The gang scattered around the sinks
and began washing the cake out of their
fur, faces and clothing. 'This shampoo
smells funky,' Bryan said, lathering up
his mane. 'And why is it so creamy?'

'Mine is the same. UGH, wait . . .'
Mona held up the bottle and her mouth
dropped open.

On the bottom of the bottle was a sticker that said: **YOU'VE BEEN PRANKED!** And a fancy signature from the founders.

'Oh, devils!' Bram grimaced. 'Please don't tell me it's hair-removal cream. I can't lose my fur!'

'No.' Mona shook her head. 'It's foot cream, according to the label underneath.'

'HAHAHAHAHA!' Sheila roared. 'Oh, my badness. You're going to smell funky all day.'

Tony groaned and dragged his hands down his face like *The Scream* painting. 'Can this day get any worse?!'

'Tony, you don't have any hair. Why

are you even using shampoo?' Sheila
asked.

'DON'T BE HAIR-IST! Bald people
like to use shampoo too,' Tony defended.

Bram grinned at his friends and an
idea popped into his head. 'C'mon, gang
– I think we need to work on impressing
the founders and getting them to notice
us.'

The fledgling villains were given a free
hour for rest and refreshments before the
start of the next task. The Cereal Killers
and their parents sat in the library,
strategically positioned around a table
beside the founders.

Bram's friends and their parents
listened to his dads' tales of their time
at school. When they first met, they

hadn't really liked each other. His dads were on opposing teams, in separate classes, and one night, during a stakeout in their Physical Escape class, Papa Percevil had decided to distract Dad Derek by planting a kiss on his cheek. The distraction worked and they created an alliance, promising to always protect each other, which had lasted until this very day. Mona and her grandma were disgusted by the sentimental story.

Beside them, a girl named Lightning Lily, with the power of lightning and thunder, was casting a cloud over her table, showing off her powers to her friends and family – and the founders. The trick worked as the founders' eyes sparkled in wonder from across the room. Sir Nevil even gave an approving nod.

'We need to do something,' Bram

whispered to his friends. 'Something evil
to impress them.'

'You should pull a prank,' Papa Percevil
said. 'They love a prank. One helped me
win the Gruesome Games back in my day.'

'Really?' Bram said in wonder, his eyes
glowing.

'I don't think anything will help you
win the Gruesome Games,' Tony's dad,
Grimm, said bluntly. 'I'm not sure this
school is even teaching you villains the

right skills to survive out in the wild.
I could teach you better myself. The
Gruesome Games are tame compared to
the real world.'

'You always were a tough nut, weren't
you, Grimm?' came a voice from behind
them. It was Sir Nevil who spoke, and all
the other founders' eyes were on them
too. 'It's good to see you after all these
years. Is this your son?'

'Good to see you too. And yes, this is

my son, Skele-tony,' Grimm replied.

Tony did an awkward shuffle in his seat. 'It's just Tony.'

Sir Nevil grinned. An evil grin filled with menace. 'Lovely to meet you, Tony. I hope you fair better in the Gruesome Games than your father did.'

'Now, that's not fair,' Grimm defended. 'I was sabotaged. By yourselves, no less. You threw the banana that made me slip in the final race!'

'Ah, yes, that old chestnut. You've always been bitter about losing the Gruesome Games, haven't you?' Zyla laughed. 'It's time to move on and let go of the grudge, Grimm. Lighten up. Have some fun!'

'A good villain never forgets,' Grimm whispered. 'C'mon, Tony. Let's get out of here.'

The Cereal Killers stared at each other awkwardly as Grimm left the table. But Tony didn't move.

'Skele-tony?! I said come *on*!' Grimm called across the room.

'No,' Tony said. 'You promised that I could finish the Gruesome Games and that's what I'm going to do.'

'I'm not going to change my mind,' Grimm said flatly as he walked back over. 'You have nothing to learn at this school any more. It's gone downhill.'

At this, the founders stood up from their seats. Sir Nevil's eyes glowed threateningly. 'Never insult Villains Academy in front of us.'

Bram bravely stood up to defuse the tension. 'Tony has to finish the Gruesome Games,' he told Grimm. 'Otherwise we're all disqualified because we won't have a full team. You don't want to ruin all of our futures, do you?'

Bram's dads, Mona's grandma, Bryan's parents and Sheila's parents all stood up in defence of their children.

'If you think you're messing up my granddaughter's education, you have another think coming. Now sit down, you bony fool,' Mona's grandma spat at Grimm. Beside her, Mona grinned with pride while Tony whispered something in Bryan's ear.

'You heard the woman,' Ser Bona Lisa told Grimm. 'Sit down.'

'Actually,' Tony said as he stood up, 'we've learnt a lot at this school. We've learnt to believe in ourselves, to trust our instincts and work as a team. Last term we even took down our ex-teacher, Felix Frostbite.'

The founders nodded. 'Yes, I remember hearing something about that,' Lord Moon Moon replied. 'Well done.'

'Well done?!' Ser Bona Lisa said. 'For devil's sake, Moon Moon. You're *supposed* to be bad, not giving out gold stars.'

'Son of a biscuit,' Lord Moon Moon replied. 'Is a villain not allowed to give a compliment any more?'

Bram smiled and thought about how he and the Cereal Killers always bickered over the smallest things.

'We're going to show you what we've learnt today, Dad,' Tony continued. 'And I'm going to prove you wrong.'

'Fighting talk. I like it!' Sir Nevil replied. 'Now, as lovely as this is, we do have some games to play. You should all be heading outside for the second task.'

The gang pushed their seats out from the table and joined their parents, who were still standing. Tony whispered hurriedly to each of the Cereal Killers in turn. He had a plan.

'It was nice to meet you,' Tony said to the founders, and shook Sir Nevil's hand before he could protest.

'LOVELY! Absolutely splendid,' Sheila said and flew through Master Masonnaise, who proceeded to chase her to the far end of the library, trying to slap her around the face.

Mona fist-
bumped Ser Bona Lisa
goodbye and Bram bowed
to Lord Moon Moon, who also
bowed in return – much to the disgust
of Zyla. Bryan walked up to Zyla and
offered his paw.

'I'm not shaking that.' Zyla frowned.

'I don't want you to shake it,' Bryan
replied. 'I want you to pull my finger.'

'HA! Like I'd fall for that one,' Zyla
replied. 'That's the oldest joke in the book.'

Bryan shrugged. 'Exactly. So why
would I be pranking you with a prank that
everyone knows? Just because you're too
much of a *chicken* to pull my finger . . .'

At the word **CHICK**EN, the founders fidgeted in their seat. Zyla's eyes shone with menace and reluctantly she reached out and pulled on Bryan's paw. As she pulled, Bryan squinted and let out a humongous fart that ripped through the library. Zyla rolled her eyes and then almost toppled off her chair at the smell. She attempted to grab her net to waft the smell away . . . only to change her mind when the methane gas reacted with her magic and began sending sparks around the library.

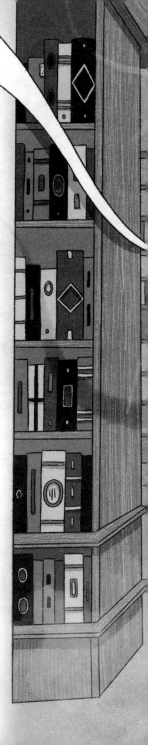

'STOP, ZYLA!' the other founders
screeched and ran around the bookshelves
to extinguish the sparks before they set
the whole library alight.

'Devils incarcerated, what
did that lion eat?' Master
Masonnaise roared as the
cloud engulfed them.

'I can't breathe! **I
CAN'T BREATHE!**'
Lord Moon Moon gasped.

'Quit being dramatic,
Moon Moon,' Ser Bona
Lisa barked.

'Oh, just
because
you don't
have any nostrils
or sense of smell!' the
wolf snapped back.

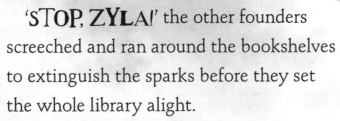

'It's fogging my brain! I can't think clearly,' Sir Nevil panted.

'And *that* is how we took down our enemy last term,' Tony shouted with a humongous grin as the Cereal Killers and their families ran out of the library and on to the grounds of Villains Academy. They'd made sure that the founders noticed them and Bram saw the look of pride on Grimm's face.

Bram was going to do all that he could to make sure they won the games to keep his friend from leaving the school.

CHAPTER 8

GRUESOME GAME TWO:

TUG OF WAR

The second Gruesome Game was held outside in the grounds of Villains Academy. A huge arena had been erected on the edge of the Wicked Woods. At the centre was a circular platform, where Bram guessed that the game would take place. Trees grew around the seats and into a canopy overhead, where sunshine sprinkled through the leaves like small orbs of fire.

A foul stench filled the air, much to the disgust of the parents and older students who filled the stands. Nevertheless, they cheered and chanted for the fledgling first years, filling the air with an electric atmosphere.

The Cereal Killers made their way to the front and took their seats on the platform, nervous to have even more people watching them this time. Bram couldn't help but think that by pranking the founders, they had got themselves in too deep and now they had even more enemies who wanted to take them down.

'It'll be fine,' Mona whispered, seeing the look on Bram's face. 'We didn't come here to lose – and Tony's future is on the line.'

Bram nodded. It *would* be fine. They had each other.

The founders of Villains Academy emerged into the arena five minutes later with expressions that looked menacing enough to destroy even the most evil villain.

'Welcome to the second Gruesome Game,' Ser Bona Lisa announced. 'For this one, you will be working in your

teams again, but this time you will battle against your teachers.'

Cheers erupted around the stadium. The teachers looked grim.

'Sir Nevil, if you could do the honours,' Master Masonnaise said, and Sir Nevil pulled a lever.

A loud creak filled the stadium and then the circular floor at the centre of the arena split in two. The foul stench that had been lingering grew stronger and washed over the audience, causing a few people to faint in shock.

Once the floor had fully retracted, it revealed a murky swamp. Almost perfectly round and littered with decaying foliage, its surface bubbled almost as if it were alive, or at least poisonous. From one end of the swamp to the other ran a long, thick rope. The sight made Bram's stomach churn.

'I present . . . Tug of War,' Zyla announced, her voice echoing around the arena. The crowd *ooooh*ed. Bram spotted his dads in the stands, with their thumbs in the air and huge smiles on their faces.

He turned away, for fear they'd distract him from his goal of winning and saving his friend from leaving the school. All Bram had ever wanted was to make them proud and let them see that he *was* a villain. Hopefully today he could do that.

'The aim of the game is simple,' Sir Nevil said. 'Each team will take one end of the rope. The first to pull their opponents into the swamp will be the winners. You must *not* let go of the rope at any point or you will forfeit your win . . . and we will throw you in the mud ourselves. Either way, the losers are getting dirty.'

Lord Moon Moon grinned. 'Teachers, go to the far end. Fledgling villains, go to the other side and wait to be called. Your names will be chosen randomly from Ser Bona Lisa's helmet. It will be three teachers against five students, as there are more students than teachers. Plus, this equals the playing field as the teachers will most likely be stronger.'

The teachers huffed and reluctantly trudged over to the far side of the bubbling swamp. Professor Pluto called Zyla a **SHUBBLEMEGUMP** on her way past, Master Mardybum complained about his dry cleaning and Matron Bones attempted to whack Sir Nevil with a bone she kept in her pocket.

The first group of students from Class D were called forward, along with three teachers: Whiz Warmbottom, the Mouldy Knight and Guru Gertrude. The founders shouted their token phrase:

'BE **BAD**, NOT **GOOD**,

AND BRING YOUR **EVIL** OUT.

BE **CUNNING** AND **WICKED**,

BE READY WHEN WE SHOUT . . .

GO!'

And then the students and teachers went to war.

But the fight didn't last long, because before Bram could even blink, Guru Gertrude and her fellow teachers flew into the air and landed in the swamp with an almighty splash.

Sheila whooped in delight. '**OH MY BADNESS!** *Incredible!* Possibly the best day of my life. Now all I need to see is Master Mardybum faceplant in that mud.'

The teachers dragged themselves out of the mud and the next groups were

ushered in. Team after team fought to avoid landing in the swamp. Three teams of teachers won in a row, which was followed by two triumphant teams of students. Parents shouted support from the stands while the founders grinned in delight at the disgusting chaos.

'The Cereal Killers,' Ser Bona Lisa shouted. 'Against . . . Chief Crabbatus, Professor Pluto and Master Mardybum.'

The gang looked at each other with wide eyes as the final name was read.

'I'm telling you, this day could not get better!' Sheila squealed.

'Our strength is in our numbers. Stick together, pull together and remember to listen to each other. We've got this,' Mona said.

'Hell, yeah, we do,' Bram said as the gang huddled their heads together.

'Think of all the times Master Mardybum has called you out or made fun of you. Or every time Chief Crabbatus threw a book at your head, or Professor Pluto called you a **SHUBBLEMEGUMP**. Now is our chance to get our revenge.'

'All right, all right, enough of the pep talk.' Zyla yawned. 'Will you hurry up? Or I'm going to declare you the losers for being slow.'

The Cereal Killers rushed forward and grabbed hold of the rope. Bram was at the front, followed by Mona, Bryan, Tony and then Sheila. *'Put the weakest at the back,'* Mona had ordered.

Master Mardybum's fiery eyes glared at them from across the swamp. Behind him was Professor Pluto, followed by Chief Crabbatus.

'BE BAD, NOT GOOD,

AND BRING YOUR EVIL OUT.

BE CUNNING AND WICKED,

BE READY WHEN WE SHOUT . . .

GO!' Master Masonnaise yelled.

The Cereal Killers pulled for their
lives. Bram's arms threatened to tear out
of their sockets and a blood vessel in his
temple felt like it would burst from the

pressure. Mona death-gripped the rope and yelled instructions at her teammates like an angry sports coach. Bryan grabbed the rope between his jaws and clenched his bum even harder, trying not to gas Tony and Sheila behind him. Tony struggled with the rope, losing the odd

finger, and fought to keep his arms from popping away from his body.

Sheila was having the time of her life. Her tail was wrapped around the rope as she sang songs in the background, apparently spurring her team on through the inspirational sound of ghostsong.

Master Mardybum pulled the rope even harder. His mind burned with willpower and he glared at the troublemakers across from him, determined to crush them so that his robes didn't get dirty.

Bram's blood boiled as Master Mardybum yelled insults at him. He tried to focus, but

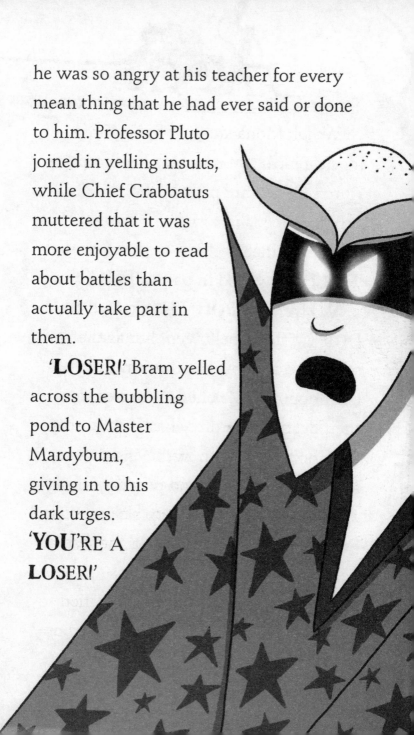

he was so angry at his teacher for every mean thing that he had ever said or done to him. Professor Pluto joined in yelling insults, while Chief Crabbatus muttered that it was more enjoyable to read about battles than actually take part in them.

'**LOSER!**' Bram yelled across the bubbling pond to Master Mardybum, giving in to his dark urges. '**YOU**'RE A **LOSER!**'

'Wow!' Mona shouted back. 'Great insult, Bram. Good to see that Professor Pluto's classes are paying off.'

Bram's feet slid forward, carrying him a few inches closer to the swamp. '**PULL!**' he yelled in panic. '**PULL!**'

'**WHAT DO YOU THINK WE'RE DOING?!**' Tony bellowed. But as the seconds ticked by, the rhythmic tug of their opponents inched them closer to their destiny of a dirty bath.

'Who's the loser now?!' Master Mardybum grinned and began yanking even harder. His eyes were bloodshot and his grip on the rope was so tight that his hands were pure white.

Slowly but surely, the Cereal Killers were being pulled towards the swamp.

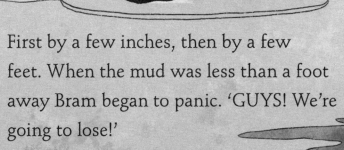

First by a few inches, then by a few feet. When the mud was less than a foot away Bram began to panic. 'GUYS! We're going to lose!'

'STOP PANICKING!' Mona shouted. 'Just focus!'

But it was no use. Bram's feet dug into the dirt and he made track marks as he was pulled closer. Master Mardybum grinned in delight, with pure evilness and menace in his expression, which only wound Bram up more. He was not going to go down quietly – and *definitely* not without getting revenge on his teacher. But the mud was only a few inches away. They were going to lose.

'You're useless, Bram! A terrible villain! A **LOSER!**' Master Mardybum shouted.

Bram saw red. In a final act of defiance, he yelled for his friends to jump and then cannonballed into the swamp. His friends followed and mud flew everywhere. The vile-smelling slop covered the teachers head to toe as the founders grinned down at them.

'My gown!' Master Mardybum roared. 'You *will* be receiving my dry-cleaning bill, Bram Moon! Mark my words!'

Bram lay in the mud beaming from ear to ear. Sure, they had just lost the second Gruesome Game. But they *had* managed to cover their teachers with mud, make the founders smile *and* pull off a fun prank. The Gruesome Games weren't about following the rules or winning the most games. There were no rules – you just had to prove your badness. And right now, Bram felt pretty badass.

CHAPTER 9

WINNER, WINNER, CHICKEN DINNER

The Cereal Killers walked back towards Villains Academy to clean up before lunch. Birds flew overhead and older students cheered as they walked by. The gang couldn't stop singing Bram's praises and were elated about angering Master Mardybum, though they had no doubt that he would get his revenge one day.

As they entered the bathroom, Bram caught sight of himself in the mirror.

He looked as if he had spent an eternity lost in the Wicked Woods and had transformed into a swamp monster. Mud caked his fur and his knitted jumper was unrecognizable.

The Cereal Killers headed for the showers and rinsed off the vile-smelling mud. Bram peeled away the dirty clothes that clung to his fur and tossed them over the cubicle door. The mud fell away as he lathered himself from head to toe in bloodfruit-and-basil-scented foaming gel, and as he stuck his face under the shower head he let himself have a moment away from the chaos.

Bram forgot about the Gruesome Games and the need to save his friend from leaving the school. He forgot about his dads and the pressure that came with them being here. He forgot about the founders and their famous *Book of Bad*. And he forgot about Villains Academy, instead focusing on his breath and the water falling over him like gentle rainfall in the spring. His chest rose and fell, calming to a normal rhythm. His shoulders relaxed, as if forgetting why they were so tense in the first place.

Then a loud yell yanked him back to reality.

'Oi! Which one of you scoundrels has stolen my clothes?!' Mona shouted.

Bram wrapped himself in a towel and rushed to see what the commotion was about. Mona was standing by the sinks, her hair dripping wet and a bathrobe wrapped tightly around her.

'It wasn't me!' insisted Tony, who was also dressed in just a towel. 'My clothes are gone too.'

Bram looked around at the floor for his own clothes. But there was nothing there. Not even a hint of muddy splatters that said they even existed. Whoever had stolen them had covered their tracks well. 'Mine are gone as well.'

'You have got to be kidding me!' Mona shrieked in panic. 'There is *no way* I'm running around the corridors naked. No way!'

'We'll find them, keep your hat on,' Tony said with a smirk.

'You should embrace the naked-ness,' Sheila smiled. 'Bryan and I have been doing it for years.'

Mona rolled her eyes. 'Well, you and Bryan can get lost. I don't want to hear your silly advice right now. I want to find my clothes and whoever has taken them so I can zap them into the next century.'

Bram looked around the room, peering into every nook and cranny. The clothes were nowhere to be seen and it soon became very clear where they had gone.

The main doors to the bathroom were locked. Hanging on the back were five chicken costumes with a small note that read:

Revenge is oh so sweet.
Who's the chicken now, losers?!
If you don't come out in these costumes then you will be splattered with slime and feathers. Either way, you're chickens.
Worst wishes,
The Founders

'It appears the founders are taking revenge for Bryan's fart,' Bram said, staring at the note and the chicken

costumes that hung
in front of him.

'Oh, for badness'
sake,' Mona sighed.
'Every waking moment
of today we're having to
watch our backs. It's never-ending!'

'That's the life of a villain,' Bram
replied and rested his hand on Mona's
shoulder. 'They're making an example
of us because we showed them up. And
personally, I'd rather wear the costumes
than be splattered with more gunk. I've
only just washed out the mud from the
Tug of War!'

'Agreed,' Mona said in defeat.

'We'll just have to style it out, Cereal Killers style! Show them that it's not a punishment. That we enjoy it.' Bram beamed. 'You can only be embarrassed if you let yourself be embarrassed. We can do it together.'

'But . . . but everyone will laugh at us,' Mona said with a crack in her voice.

'So let them laugh,' Bram said with a shrug and a supportive smile. 'If the worst they can do is laugh while we're having fun, then that's okay.'

'But I've never let anyone see me embarrassed. I've always put on a brave face.' Mona shuffled her feet and cast her eyes down. 'My parents didn't like me showing emotion, so I learnt to hide it. It's embarrassing that everyone's parents are here today and mine aren't. Though

I am grateful my grandma came.'

'Let them laugh,' Bram said with a squeeze of Mona's hand. 'You already have your family around you today and we're going to do this together. If your parents could see you, they'd be proud. There's nothing to be embarrassed about – we're going to have fun!'

'When did our roles reverse? Thank you, Bram. For being my be—' Mona stopped herself. 'My friend.'

Bram smiled. Was she about to say *best friend*? 'Let's do this, then!' he said.

The gang pulled on their costumes. Huge hoods covered their heads and tips of pointy beaks hung over their foreheads. Yellow feathers covered their bodies, making them look like feather dusters, and bright orange boots housed their feet.

They looked ridiculous. But they were determined to make the most of it.

As soon as their costumes were on, the doors magically clicked open. The gang sauntered through the halls without a care in the world . . . Well, that's what their expressions told the world. Inside, they were all dying from embarrassment.

They held their heads high and detoured through the kitchens, which were still completely wrecked from the first Gruesome Game, to grab eggs to use as weapons. They threw them at their teachers and chased fellow students through the corridors, threatening to peck them to death. Sheila attempted to tickle people with her feathers and Bryan swore that he could make himself fly if he farted hard enough.

When the gang burst into the food hall

for lunch, parents gawped and pointed. Whispers echoed around the room, but the friends stuck together as a flock and barged aside anyone who stood in their path.

The founders watched with their eyes narrowed in suspicion as the Cereal Killers flaunted their feathers. Bram gave the founders a wave, while Tony launched an egg in their direction.

Papa Percevil looked confused at Bram and his friends as they approached their table. 'What's going on?'

Bram managed to smile, but his

confidence disappeared and his words choked in his throat. He thought that he was brave, but when it came to his dads, he wasn't so sure that he was as bad as they wanted him to be.

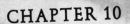

CHAPTER 10

GRUESOME GAME THREE:

THE HEAD-AND-SPOON RACE

After lunch had been eaten and everyone's bellies were satisfyingly full, the Cereal Killers changed into their normal clothes before the founders of Villains Academy announced the final Gruesome Game.

'The final game of the day will be the Head-and-Spoon Race,' Sir Nevil announced as he and the founders stood by the main doors. 'We thought about holding it in the arena, but had a change of heart. The arena isn't quite *deadly* or special enough for the one-hundredth anniversary.'

Tony's dad, Grimm, grinned at the mention of death, but Tony grimaced. 'Yikes.'

'So, to mark this special occasion, we have decided to hold the game in the forbidden graveyard,' Master Masonnaise said. 'If you could all make your way outside.'

'The forbidden graveyard?!' Mal from the Overlords shouted out. 'But no student is allowed to enter it?! We've been warned that if we set one foot in there then evil spirits will throw us out. Or worse, monsters will eat us!'

'Exactly. Much more deadly.' Ser Bona Lisa smiled. 'Which is why you won't be able to touch the floor.'

'Easy peasy.' Sheila grinned.

'How are we supposed to complete the game if we can't touch the floor?' Mal protested. 'This is unfair!'

'Life is unfair,' Zyla said, rolling her eyes. 'If you can make your way outside like you've been told, then you'll see how to complete it, annoying boy.'

Lord Moon Moon skipped over the grass in delight as they headed out on to the grounds. 'Oh, this is going to be the most epic game of "the floor is lava" you have ever seen!'

The entrance to the forbidden graveyard looked the same as it did this morning. Eerie and full of swirling mist so that most of the graveyard itself was obscured from view. Bram dreaded to think about what lurked inside.

Huge rocks and other obstacles had been put in place so the students could take multiple routes around the gravestones and from where the Cereal Killers were standing, it looked relatively easy.

'The game is simple,' Ser Bona Lisa said, her voice echoing over the grass as the afternoon sun dipped low in the sky. 'You will be given a spoon and a head. Most likely the head of a wrackwurt, a sniggle, a pondato or a fugglewuggle. You must get across the forbidden graveyard and cross the finish line at the other end. You *must* have a head when you cross the finish line and you mustn't touch the ground. There will be obstacles, rocks and other objects for you to use to get across.'

'If you touch the ground, you'll be escorted back to the gates at the entrance to the graveyard by some very unfriendly ghosts,' Lord Moon Moon said with an evil grin. 'Meaning you'll have to start the race again.'

'Now, come grab a spoon and a head,' said Zyla. 'Don't worry, they don't bite.'

Students rushed forward to grab their heads and spoons, eager to start the final Gruesome Game. The Cereal Killers grabbed theirs, and Bram stared at them in disgust, trying not to bring up his lunch. He'd been given the head of a wrackwurt – a weird purple creature with big ears, three huge nostrils, a nose wart and two closed eyes. His main reason for choosing it was that it was smaller than the rest, and presumably easier to balance. It snored quietly and Bram hoped that it would stay asleep. But the worst part was that the spoons were *tiny*. Anyone would struggle to balance a sprout on them, never mind a massive head.

Parents and older students took their seats on the walls around the forbidden graveyard. They cheered and chanted, clapping in a rhythm like a war march, eager for the final Gruesome Game to begin.

'Right, Sheila, because you can fly, you're going to be our eyes,' Mona instructed. 'You don't need to touch the ground, but you can't win without us. We're going to need you to fly ahead and guide the rest of us.'

'Deal!' Sheila said as she swallowed both her head and spoon, which jiggled around in her belly.

'How are we going to balance the head?' Bram asked. 'I'm going to drop it. The spoon is so small!'

'Shove it up the nostril,' Mona said with a wink. Bram grimaced in disgust, but admitted that this was a good tactic. After all, there were no rules, and cheating was encouraged, so this was a good way for Bram to make sure he had both the head and spoon when he crossed the finish line.

'Come on, come on! Gather round, we haven't got all day,' Sir Nevil shouted and pushed students towards the archway to the graveyard. The ornate gates were flung open, gaping almost two metres wide, daring visitors to enter. The Cereal Killers barged their way to the front, along with the Overlords, who pushed and shoved people out of their way.

The founders rubbed their hands together with sinister expressions, and for the last time chanted:

'BE **BAD**, NOT **GOOD**,

AND BRING **YOUR EVIL** OUT.

BE **CUNNING** AND **WICKED**,

BE READY WHEN WE SHOUT . . .

GO!'

Students rushed forward and forced themselves through the gates. Some hopped on to stepping stones. Others walked on stilts that were provided. Some fell to the ground, which caused angry ghosts to rise from the gravestones and toss them back over the wall to the starting line. Parents and guardians sat on the high walls surrounding the graveyard, screaming for their children to do well, while the founders flew around pranking the students.

HELP!

They tickled students'
armpits and tripped
them up using invisible
wire, causing most of the
fledgling villains to tumble.

Creature heads rolled on
the ground. Spoons were
used as swords as students
fought over whose head was whose
while the heads snapped at their fingers.

Bram shoved the spoon up the
wrackwurt's nostril, causing it to
pass out, and focused on where he
was stepping. He jumped on to stones
covered in slippery moss, meaning he
had to firmly plant his feet or face the
wrath of the ghosts. He hopped from
one rock to another, until he reached a
dead end seven stones in.

'Where do I go, Sheila?!' Bram shouted,

looking around for his friend in the misty sky. But she was nowhere to be seen and the students behind him were growing impatient.

'Come on! Move! You're blocking the way!' a girl behind him shouted, before she went flying off her stone. Behind her was Mal, who had his arms stretched out and was happily pushing anyone in his way – and he was heading straight for Bram. He jumped towards Bram's stone and shoved him so hard that Bram toppled to the floor.

Within seconds an angry ghoul emerged from the grave beside him and picked him up. *'Do not enter this sacred ground again!'* the ghost roared as it threw Bram back to the starting line.

Bram landed with a **THUMP.** The idea of having to start the course again made him panic and he prayed that his dads couldn't see him. He looked around for his friends and soon realized that he wasn't alone. In fact, the majority of the first years were gathered by the gates of the graveyard, either too afraid to enter or tired of being tossed back to the start. This made Bram feel a little better.

'Come on, Bram!' Mona shouted as she landed on her bum beside him. 'There's no time to waste.'

She pushed Bram through the gates and began hopping over obstacles and gravestones. Spikes jutted out at angles to stop them. Weeds and vines grew from the ground to grab their legs. But they didn't let that stop them – not with Sheila flying around screaming directions to help them avoid the worst obstacles.

Mona followed in Bram's wake as he concentrated on not falling over.

He heard his dads shouting his name in the distance, but tried to block them out. Thinking about them now would definitely make him mess up. He wanted to win the Gruesome Games for them. To carry on the victorious tradition of the Moon family. He couldn't do that if he was on the ground.

The Tooth Hairy stood ahead of them, her hair flying out at all angles, taking down anyone who tried to pass her. 'Oh, look who it is,' she sneered and attempted to grab Bram's leg. But Bram was too fast, and batted her away with his head and spoon.

'Oh, will you MOVE, sonny peep!' Sheila screeched and then flew straight through the Tooth Hairy's head, giving her such a bad brain freeze that she toppled over like a statue. Roots burst from the ground, grabbed her from all sides and dragged her back to the starting line.

'**GO, GO, GO!**' Sheila ordered. Bram didn't need telling twice and rushed forward. Mona followed. Bryan was on stilts not far behind, with Tony sat on his back like he was riding him into battle.

The gang moved through the mist

as quickly as they could, careful not
to drop their heads or spoons or touch
the ground. Students screamed in the
distance and occasionally they saw a
founder fly by. Gravestones appeared
out of nowhere and figures lurked in the

shadows, waiting to grab them. But the Cereal Killers didn't stop long enough to let anything touch them.

'There!' Bram shouted. 'The finish line, I see it!'

'Go, Bram, go!' Mona whooped.

The watchful parents and older students whooped louder. Their cheers split Bram's eardrums as the excitement grew. Students moved through the mist around them, all aiming to be the first to cross the finish line. Bram focused on his goal of saving his friend from leaving the school and making his parents proud. Of achieving a dream for them, for himself. His feet bashed the stones as he hopped and jumped with grace.

But the Overlords weren't going to let them win. Particularly Mal. He was fed up of the Cereal Killers always taking the glory – always outdoing the Overlords somehow. He eyed Bram with menace from a few gravestones over and launched a rogue snapping head through the air – straight at the werewolf's face.

Bram heard it before he saw it. The jaws gnashed as they grew closer. He held up his wrackwurt head and spoon to defend himself and it was torn from his grasp as they fought and fell to the ground along with the spoon. A bony hand burst out of the soil and launched the heads through the air like footballs.

'NOOOO!' Bram shouted as he watched his hopes and dreams disappear.

'We need to move!' Mona urged. 'There's a swarm of people coming up behind and they'll push us off to get past.'

But Bram refused to go. 'I can't cross the finish line without a head. We can't win. I've ruined it for all of us. I'm so sorry, Tony!'

The Cereal Killers looked at each other in horrified realization. But Tony wasn't giving in. 'I am **NOT** leaving this school. Take my head!' he shouted. 'The founders didn't specify in the rules *which* head it had to be, just that you must have one. **JUST TAKE MY HEAD!**'

Sheila unscrewed Tony's skull and plonked it in Bram's arms. Bram placed the spoon in Tony's mouth and then ran towards the finish line. He thanked

Tony for saving his skin and thought about how grateful he was to have these misfits as friends. It wouldn't be the same if one of them had to leave.

But while the Cereal Killers were stalling, the Overlords passed the finish line in a blur and the crowd went wild. Bram cursed loudly as they crossed just after them and Mal shook his head and spoon in their faces. 'Victory is sweet, losers!' the Overlords shouted.

Shame hit Bram in the face. He'd really thought that they could win and save their friend from leaving the school. But he'd ruined it by dropping his wrackwurt head. He was disappointed with himself and was sure his parents would be too. The founders laughed.

'Hard luck,' Sir Nevil said with a shrug.

Mona eye-rolled. Bryan and Sheila hugged Tony and screwed his head back on while the Overlords shouted

'**LOOOOOSERS!**'

Bram looked away in embarassment and then ran as fast as he could away from his problems.

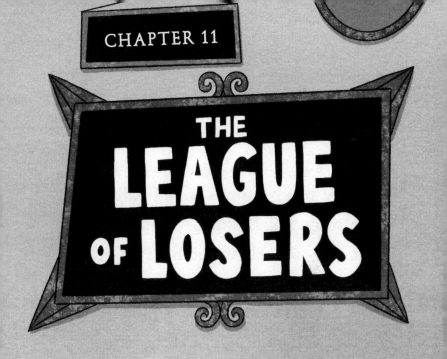

CHAPTER 11

THE LEAGUE OF LOSERS

Bram felt like a loser. The Overlords thought he was one. His dads probably thought it, too. He ran back to Villains Academy wishing that the ground would swallow him up.

Tears flowed down his cheeks and dripped off his chin like a waterfall. He'd failed to fulfil his dads' dream of winning the Gruesome Games and had sealed his friend Tony's fate. He had never felt worse in his life.

He pelted through the corridors without thinking. Statues whizzed past in a blur and booby traps missed him by inches. When his limbs were finally tired and his mind had calmed, Bram slowed down to a stop. He wiped his eyes but couldn't work out which floor he was on. The walls were lined with the usual portraits and paintings, and the carpet was just as luxurious as everywhere else. The only thing different was the statue beside him.

The statue of Sir Nevil. It towered over him, its stone eyes burning into his soul. Bram felt a sudden rush of hatred and decided to use the cape around the statue's neck to blow his nose on. It was a small and petty revenge, but one that filled him with much joy.

But the pleasure didn't last very long. It soon turned into pure terror as the statue craned its neck down towards Bram and *bowed* to him.

Bram screamed in fright, falling back on to the floor. *Statues shouldn't move! Is this another of the founders' pranks?* he thought.

He looked around the corridor, wondering if he would see a head poking from a doorway, and listened out for a distant snigger, but there was nobody. He was all alone.

Then
came a loud **CLICK**
and the statue began to
move. Its head tilted upright and
the whole thing slid back *into* the wall,
revealing an ornate stone archway.

Beyond the archway was nothing but darkness, and yet this didn't scare Bram. Something about it seemed familiar, as if he had been waiting for this to happen. But he couldn't explain why.

Without hesitating, Bram pulled himself to his feet and walked through the mysterious opening. The air was cool and the darkness surrounded him as he moved forward. The statue behind him slid back into place, shutting him in, yet Bram wasn't afraid.

At the end of the tunnel the archway opened up into a huge circular room. It looked like a common room, filled with opulent furniture made of solid wood and soft velvet upholstery. High-backed armchairs were surrounded by coffee tables, piles of books and cosy candles. At the far end of the room was a huge fireplace, which housed an enormous crest that Bram didn't recognize. His eyes followed stairs which led to other levels and above it all was a beautiful ceiling covered with the finest paintwork of a sky he had ever seen. Orbs of light bobbed through the air, floating as if they didn't have a care in the world.

The carpets were soft under Bram's feet and the deep pile sank as he walked further into the room. He eyed a 3D model of Villains Academy and the

grounds, which captured the Wicked Woods in all its beautifully spooky detail. Weapons and bookshelves decorated the walls – and there were books everywhere! Bram wanted nothing more than to curl up in an armchair and read something good. It was as if he had been transported to a long-lost world.

And yet, none of it *seemed* lost. The surfaces weren't coated with dust, and the air didn't smell stale. It was as if this place had been kept in a time capsule away from the rest of the school.

'I see you've found our lair,' said a voice.

Bram jumped and spun on his heel. Sir Nevil was standing in the archway staring back at him.

Bram struggled to speak. He hadn't meant to break in! He'd found this place by accident.

'It's okay,' Sir Nevil said, his expression calm. 'This is the headquarters of the League of Losers.'

'The what?' Bram mumbled.

'The League of Losers. It's a secret society for special villains – misfits, outcasts, rebels. Those who find it hard to fit in and need help to find their place in the world. It's a community, built for us to bond with each other at Villains Academy. I set it up when we built the school,' Sir Nevil said, perching on one of the armchairs by the fire. 'I like to come back to visit the place every time I return. It's the nostalgia.'

'But you're so mean,' Bram replied honestly.

'I wasn't always this mean,' Sir Nevil chuckled. 'Nobody is born mean . . . bad . . . evil. Whatever you want to

call it. Nobody is born *anything*. We're
all a product of our upbringing, of
our surroundings, our families and
our education. Everyone has different
problems and circumstances in their life
– but nobody is born evil. It's a choice.
One that you have to make. And the
fact that you're here at Villains Academy
means that you've already made that
choice, which is great. You're on the
path to becoming a real villain. But why

should being slightly smaller, shy, timid, anxious or different mean you can't be a true villain?! Some people need a little extra help sometimes and that's okay. Devil knows I did.' Sir Nevil closed his eyes and took a deep breath.

Bram watched the famous founder and felt horrible for ever thinking the worst of him. People weren't always exactly how they seemed.

Bram made himself comfy in an armchair. 'I wasn't born bad either,' he said. 'I feel like a bit of a loser, actually.'

Sir Nevil smiled. 'I've been watching you today and I agree. I think you're a loser.'

Bram's heart dropped. Surely Sir Nevil wasn't supposed to agree. Wasn't he supposed to be nice and say the opposite?

The shock must have showed on his

face because Sir Nevil's smile widened. 'Being a loser is one of the best things you can ever be in your life. Once you accept that you're a loser, nobody can ever put you down again. How can they?! You have already accepted it – so now you use it as a strength. Being different is a huge strength and there's power in following your own path. *So what* if your brain works differently to everyone else's or you don't enjoy the things that are "normal" to enjoy. We're all losers. All of us! Every single person in this world is a loser!'

Bram smiled. 'Why are you a loser?'

'I'm rubbish at pranking,' Sir Nevil said. 'Most of the pranks I'm famous for were actually pulled off by my dear friend Zyla. Though don't tell anyone that because it's not cool or villainous to have a best friend. I only ever tried to pull off one prank by myself – and that ended up being a total embarrassment!'

'The moustache drawing?' Bram said quietly.

'Yes, that's the one!' Sir Nevil laughed. 'I couldn't finish it, and I lost my own moustache to Zyla's hair-remover prank. After that, I had to ask her for help to get my reputation back. But it's okay. We all have strengths and weaknesses. If I'm honest, I don't actually like pranking that much. I much prefer plotting.'

'Me too,' Bram agreed.

'You do know it's okay that you didn't win any of the games today, don't you?' Sir Nevil said. 'They're not the be-all and end-all of your time at Villains Academy, they're just a bit of fun. I actually think that you're going to go on to do much greater things, Bram. I set up the *Book of Bad* to document the winners of the Gruesome Games. So that we can remember and celebrate those who are best at being evil. But there are other ways for you to get your name in there . . .' The founder winked.

'Really?' Bram said hopefully, his spirits rising. 'Would you also happen to know how I can change Grimm's mind about Villains Academy? Asking for a friend.'

'Oh, he's not as hard on the inside as you might think,' Sir Nevil said. 'Why don't you show him this?' He handed Bram a small silver skull-shaped pin badge that had the letters L.O.L. engraved into it.

'What's this?' Bram asked.

'A token you can keep, as an official member of the League of Losers. Do you accept the invitation to become a loser?'

Bram stood up from his chair with a smile. 'I do.'

Sir Nevil clapped his hands. 'Marvellous! You are now officially a loser – along with many other students and teachers who I'm sure you'll meet in the coming weeks. It's quite a big group.'

'Can my friends become losers too?' Bram asked in wonder.

'You mustn't talk about the League of Losers with anyone, Bram,' Sir Nevil warned. 'It's a well-kept secret. The league will call them if and when the time is right. Or an acting teacher or founder can enrol them.'

'Okay.' Bram nodded. It was going

to be hard to keep this secret from his friends, but he was hopeful that one day they could join the league too. And that there was a way to fix the mess he'd made today. 'There's something I want to do as my first act as a loser.'

'And what's that?' Sir Nevil asked.

'I want to play a prank,' Bram said with an evil grin. He had a plan to cheer up his friends, impress Grimm *and* make his dads proud.

CHAPTER 12

THE PRANK OF A LIFETIME

Bram explained that he wanted to help pull off Sir Nevil's centuries-old prank of drawing moustaches on everyone and everything. Except this time with a twist that nobody would see coming. It was going to be difficult, but Bram believed that they could do it.

The first step was to get rid of his dads. They insisted on keeping him company, but Bram sent them on a wild goose chase

to find him some cake to cheer him up.
He felt bad about tricking his parents, but
it was for a *bad* cause: to pull off the prank
with Sir Nevil. The Cereal Killers on the
other hand were easy to avoid. Bram was
sure that they hated him for making them
lose the final Gruesome Game.

Bram and Sir Nevil set the wheels
in motion. First, they broke into the
greenhouse to steal the batches of
invisible ink Class Z had made yesterday.
Bram thought this would be an easy step,
but since the accident during his first
week at the school, where Furyflumps
had been stolen, the security around the

greenhouse had been increased.

Thin wires that triggered alarms ran around the trees. Bram hopped over them like a ballerina and gracefully danced his way to the back doors. Sir Nevil floated through them without a care in the world.

'How do you do that?' Bram asked. 'Aren't you solid?'

'I can choose if I want to be transparent or solid.' Sir Nevil shrugged. 'One perk of being an immortal legend.'

'Then why am I tiptoeing around here like an idiot when you could float in there and get the ink without me?' Bram said.

'And what would be fun about that?'
Sir Nevil replied and purposely trod on
an alarm wire.

Sirens burst into Bram's eardrums,
almost knocking him off his feet. His
brain felt like it was caving in on itself
and it took all his willpower to pick the
lock of the greenhouse door. As soon
as it clicked, Bram pushed through the
doors with all of his strength, desperate
to get away from the screaming that
blocked his thoughts. Though if Master
Mardybum caught him in here he would
be dead meat, which was the last thing
he needed right now.

Bram attempted to calm his nerves as
he ran to the jars of invisible ink that sat
on the counter, their contents swirling
like glittery moon juice. It was as if
they were alive and somehow magical.

Without wasting any precious seconds, Bram swept them into his arms and turned back to the exit.

But a figure stood in the doorway, blocking his path.

The silhouette wore a gown with long, billowing sleeves and its eyes burned red. 'Who *DARES* enter my greenhouse without permission?!' Master Mardybum roared.

Bram ducked, almost dropping the jars. He shuffled around huge plants and under tables, desperate to find an exit.

Master Mardybum swept around the room, peering into every nook and cranny in search of the thief. His shadow loomed closer and his footsteps grew louder as Bram tried to hide under the leaves of a towering brintle plant.

Bram watched the teacher's feet approach until they were mere steps away from his hiding place. The jig was up and Bram prepared his excuses, hoping and praying that he wouldn't be kicked out of Villains Academy for stealing. But before Master Mardybum had a chance to move the leaf, Sir Nevil floated through the wall on the other side of the room and coughed loudly, diverting the teacher's attention.

'You always were easy to wind up, Mardybum,' Sir Nevil taunted. 'I was just having a look around. I like what you've done with the place.'

'Sir Nevil.' Master Mardybum blushed.
'Not a problem at all. Please, take your
time. I can give you a tour if you like?'

Bram looked around for an exit. As if
evil luck was on
his side, a window
to his left was
ajar, so he made
his great escape.
One by one,
he lowered the
jars through the
window, then as
quietly and quickly

as he could, he dragged himself through
the opening. As the fresh air hit him,
Bram let out a deep sigh of relief before
collecting the jars in his arms and
running back to Villains Academy.

Meanwhile, back in the greenhouse, Sir Nevil replied blandly to Master Mardybum, 'I'll pass on a tour, actually.' The founder then walked straight through the teacher. As he did, his fingers brushed Mardybum's upper lip and Sir Nevil expertly drew a moustache in invisible ink on his face. 'See you at the midnight feast?'

'Absolutely.' Mardybum nodded in confusion. 'Have a lovely evening.'

Sir Nevil walked out of the greenhouse without a backwards glance and glided towards the school where Bram was waiting for him.

'That was close!' Bram said. 'Let's get painting moustaches!'

Bram and Sir Nevil worked their way around the school for almost an hour, painting moustaches on the hundreds

of portraits that covered the
walls. Some inhabitants of
the frames took it in their

stride, while
others attempted to bite the
pranksters' fingers off.

'I'm not sure we're going
to be able to do all of this
before the midnight feast
tonight,' Sir Nevil pondered. 'We still
need to start drawing on the teachers

and students –
which will be
even harder
when they
can *move* and
see us coming
towards their
faces with
ink.'

'Yeah, I've only managed to get two students so far by pretending to wipe dirt off their faces. And they weren't happy that I was touching them,' Bram said.

'I think we're going to need some help,' Sir Nevil said, realizing what a big task they had set for themselves.

'What about our fellow losers?' Bram grinned, excited about meeting the other members of the secret society.

'No, it's too late,' Sir Nevil replied. 'We'll never get the message around and everyone organized in time.'

'Then what about my friends? They could help. And I know we can trust them,' Bram said.

'Okay, but no mention of the losers,' Sir Nevil agreed.

Bram nodded and grinned wickedly before painting a ginormous moustache

on the portrait of an old headmaster,
who screamed that he was a
SHUBBLEMEGUMP!

Bram was nervous about seeing the
Cereal Killers and considered not asking
for help. But Sir Nevil was right, they
needed all the help they could get if they
were going to successfully prank *everyone*.

'I'm sorry I made us lose the final
game,' Bram said to his friends as he
looked at his feet to avoid eye contact.
'I shouldn't have dropped my head and
spoon. I know I ruined it for all of us and
let you down. But I think I have a way of
making it up to you.'

'What are you talking about?' Mona
replied in confusion. 'You haven't let
anyone down. They're just games – and

we had fun! Is that really what you think about us after all this time? That we're upset with you? That we don't like you?'

'Sometimes.' Bram shrugged.

'Get over yourself.' Mona rolled her eyes. 'We're all here to be villains and learn to be bad – and today we have learnt a lot, while also having a lot of fun! We're all winners, if you ask me.'

'But the Overlords called me a loser,' Bram said quietly.

'They called us *all* losers,' Mona said. 'It wasn't aimed just at you. You have serious main character syndrome.'

'And you're sure you're not mad at me?' Bram asked.

'Oh, will you **SHUSH**!' Mona shouted before squeezing Bram into a massive hug. Bryan, Sheila and Tony all joined in.

'But, out of curiosity, how are you

going to make it up to us?' Sheila asked. 'I hope it's cake.'

Bram grinned. 'No, we're going to play another prank . . .'

The Cereal Killers worked their way through Villains Academy with the invisible ink. To nobody's surprise, everyone hated their faces being touched so the gang had to get creative. Sheila mastered drawing on students' faces by flying through their heads – a trick she had learnt from Sir Nevil. Tony lost his bones and made people help put him back together – while grabbing their faces and drawing curly moustaches over them. Bryan with his big paws was no good at discreetly painting, and ran through the halls in fear when Professor Pluto sussed what he was up to and threatened to whack him with a dictionary.

Bram pretended to wipe food off Chief Crabbatus's face to draw an invisible moustache on him, while Mona shamelessly shocked people with her electric net, which left them stunned just long enough for her to draw a moustache across their upper lip. Her crowning achievement was outsmarting Zyla, who she entangled with both of their magical nets, causing an explosion of shocks that allowed her to draw on a moustache with ease. After being released, Zyla mumbled something about destroying children and told Mona to bog off.

The remaining founders were pretty easy to trick. Lord Moon Moon allowed Bryan to tickle the fur under his chin, which gave the lion a

chance to draw a moustache above the giant wolf's lip. Tony took on Master Masonnaise as he refilled his condiments – apparently he had lost a lot of his sauce throughout the day from slapping fledgling villains around the face. He then proceeded to slap Tony around the face for invading his personal space. But Tony took it on the chin, literally, and walked away with a smile as invisible ink dripped off his finger.

Sir Nevil decided to wrestle Ser Bona Lisa and stamped her with a moustache in a deadly dip. She screamed and said that if he wished to live

SLAP!

another thousand years then he would quit practising his dance moves on her.

By the time the clock struck ten, the entire school was filled with invisible moustaches, and Sir Nevil had captured the moonflies from the library for the grand unveiling at the midnight feast. The gang walked back to their dormitory to get changed.

'It was nice being friends with you all,' Tony said. 'I know we're not going to win the Trouble Trophy, but I'm glad that my last night at Villains Academy will end with a bang.'

Mona, Sheila and Bryan all gave Tony a hug and attempted to reassure him. But Bram wasn't worried about losing his friend because he had the perfect plan for how to deal with Death.

CHAPTER 13
MIDNIGHT FAREWELL FEAST

Dressed in their smart clothes, the Cereal Killers entered the food hall together to say goodbye to the founders. Bram wore his favourite knitted jumper, much to his dads' delight. Mona wore her usual hat and a smart top, while Tony had donned a long cape that made everyone around him run away in terror – because he looked exactly like his father, Grimm.

Tony's father was in his usual foul

mood, but that didn't stop Bram from sitting next to him.

'Have you always been bad?' Bram asked, while filling his plate with a pile of roast potatoes as his dads chatted to Mona's grandma. Exquisite dishes of food filled the table and steam rose through the air, obscuring the stars in the ceiling above. Moonlight shone through the windows as the clock ticked closer to midnight.

'What do you mean?' Grimm asked.

Bram thought that if Death had eyebrows, he would definitely be frowning at him right now. 'I mean, have you always been evil?'

'Death isn't evil,' Grimm replied. 'Death is inevitable.'

'But you attended Villains Academy to become a villain?' Bram said. 'So you

wanted to be evil?'

'Yes and no. You can view me however you like – to some I'm the villain, to others I'm not. Please yourself.' Grimm shrugged.

'But you want Tony to be a villain?' Bram asked.

'Of course,' Grimm replied, getting irritated. 'But he's clearly learning nothing at this school, which is why he won't be staying.'

'Is that what you did? Give up?' Bram said nonchalantly, shoving a roast potato in his mouth.

'I beg your pardon?' Grimm replied.

Bram swallowed. 'You were a loser at school. Were you not?'

'I beg your pardon?!' Tony's dad snapped. 'Do you know who I am?'

'Yes.' Bram smiled and flashed his League of Losers badge. 'A loser.'

Grimm stared at the badge with a blank face as memories hit him. 'I didn't realize the league was still going,' he whispered. 'I learnt most of my tricks there. They taught me much more than some of the teachers did.'

'It's still going strong.' Bram nodded. 'And your son is a great young villain. I've never met anyone with guts like him. He's one of my best friends and he has taught me so much since starting at Villains Academy. I think you're wrong to make him leave.'

'It's for the best,' Grimm replied.

'No, I think it's what's best for you,' Bram said. 'Because *you* didn't excel at school you're worried he will follow the same path and be a loser too. But you need to let him find his own way, his own future. He's an incredible villain.'

Before Grimm could reply, the founders stood up from their seats to make a speech. 'Thank you for another wonderful Gruesome Games – we are never disappointed with the level of evil Villains Academy produces,' Sir Nevil said. 'Now, it's time to announce the winning team, the recipients of the Trouble Trophy – and enter their names in the *Book of Bad*!'

'A drum-roll, please.' Lord Moon Moon cheered as the students stomped their feet.

Bram closed his eyes and crossed his fingers, toes, legs and everything else he could. He prayed he would hear the Cereal Killers' names.

'The winners are . . . the Overlords!' Zyla announced, and the room erupted into cheers. The Overlords screeched in delight, leapt out of their seats and hurried to collect the Trouble Trophy. The Cereal Killers rolled their eyes and turned away. Bram looked at his friend Tony, whose face was full of sadness. Mona gripped her fork tightly while whispering insults about her enemies to her grandma, who encouraged her to repeat them louder. Sheila was busy stuffing herself with cake while Bryan roared loudly in protest.

'Marvellous evilness and tactics!'
Sir Nevil praised the Overlords as he
ushered them back to their seats. 'Now,
before we end . . . I *moustache* you all a
question.'

The crowd looked at the founder in
confusion. Sir Nevil gave Bram a wink
before turning off the lights.

The food hall was plunged into
darkness. Screams filled the air as Bram

and the Cereal Killers jumped from their seats and released jars of moonflies around the room. Their blue glow filled the hall with an eerie light as they floated through the air like fireflies and the light made the whites of everyone's eyes stand out like stars in the night sky.

But they weren't the only thing that glowed . . . Shiny moustaches burned on everyone's faces.

'Do you like your moustaches?' Sir Nevil laughed as the founders began chasing him around the hall. Screeches of delight came from the founders as they ducked and dived around tables. Students rubbed their upper lips in disbelief and the Cereal Killers all high-fived each other, pleased to have helped Sir Nevil pull off his famous prank.

Grimm shook his head, shocked that someone had somehow painted a moustache on him – and complained that it had turned to a bogey-like consistency. Tony laughed and apologized to his dad. 'You were actually quite easy to prank,' Tony said.

Grimm smiled for the first time today. 'You little rascal. You're going to be hard work, aren't you?'

'Absolutely.' Tony nodded.

'I'm sorry for being so harsh on you today,' Grimm said. 'I'm not going to make you leave Villains Academy. I can see that you're learning a lot and becoming your own person and following your own path – and I'm proud of you for that.' He gave a nod to Bram, who smiled back.

Tony's face split into a humongous grin and he wrapped his arms around Grimm. 'Thank you, Dad.'

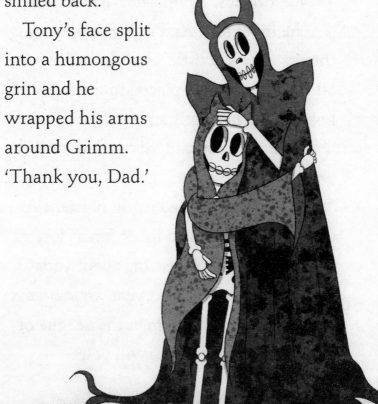

As the room settled down and everyone finished their desserts, Sir Nevil came over to say thank you.

'The founders are impressed.' Sir Nevil smiled. 'Thank you for your help and for being the evil mastermind behind the scheme, Bram.'

'No problem,' Bram said. 'It was fun.'

'The most fun! And as a way of saying thanks, I have a little something for you.' Sir Nevil discreetly placed four League of Losers badges into Bram's palm.

'Really?' Bram said, his eyes wide with wonder.

'Your friends earned it,' Sir Nevil said. 'I think you'll all have a lot of fun as losers. I'll look forward to hearing about your evil antics. See you next year. Oh, and say hi to Master Mardybum at the League of Losers meetings for me, will you?'

'Master Mardybum?!' Bram blurted out in shock.

'There are a lot more losers at Villains Academy than you think.' Sir Nevil winked as he walked away.

Master Mardybum was heading straight towards Bram. 'Are my ears burning?' he asked. 'Why did you shout my name?'

'No reason,' Bram muttered. '*Loser.*'

Master Mardybum's eyes narrowed as he sat down next to Bram. 'Rule number one is that we don't talk about it.'

'About what?' Bram asked, trying not to smirk.

'Exactly.' Mardybum nodded. 'Rule number two: every member of L.O.L. has their name written in the back of the *Book of Bad* in invisible ink – it doesn't react with Sir Nevil's protective charms. So don't let the Overlords' win get to you too much. Your name will also go down in history.'

Bram's mouth dropped open in shock.

'Rule number three,' Mardybum continued. 'Break into my greenhouse again and you'll be on the wrong end of my knitting needles, understood?'

'Don't know what you're talking about.' Bram shrugged.

'Indeed. You did a great job today, all of you,' Master Mardybum said, addressing the rest of the Cereal Killers as they sat around the table. 'Bryan, your farting prank on the founders was ingenious. And for that, I think you deserve Villain of the Week. It's about time that bum of yours earned you something. First destroying Felix Frostbite, and now this.'

Bryan was so surprised as he munched on a mouthful of sausages that he let off a round of victory farts. His proud parents joined him in his celebration farts, much to the dissatisfaction of their neighbours.

Master Mardybum quickly evacuated the room and went to save Zyla from Guru Gertrude, who was on the verge of zapping her with her magical net.

At a few minutes before midnight, the school descended on to the lawn outside as the founders left for their graves on the grounds of Villains Academy. They didn't turn back, wave or say goodbye as the clock struck midnight. Instead, they left silently like the legends they were, disappearing through the midnight mist into the forbidden graveyard.

Bram felt at peace, knowing that he was, and would always be, a true villain whether everyone thought he was or not. And what an honour it was to have met the founders of Villains Academy! But even better than that, he was a loser – in the legendary League of Losers, no less, and nothing could stop Bram's heart from swelling with pride as he said goodbye to his dads.

'I'm sorry I didn't win the Gruesome Games for you,' Bram said.

'You didn't have to do it for us, silly,' Papa Percevil said. 'And it's not always about winning, it's about having fun. With the friends you've made at Villains Academy, I think you've won anyway.'

Bram smiled and attempted to hold in a laugh as Mona and her grandma pretended to be sick behind them.

'**BYEEEEEEEEEEE!**' the Cereal Killers screamed as they waved goodbye to their families, who were getting into their skull-shaped carriages ready to leave Villains Academy.

'What a day!' Sheila wailed.

'Shall we head to the campervan for

a late-night game of exploding snap before bed?' Mona suggested.

'Actually, I don't feel like going to the campervan tonight. I have something to show you instead,' Bram said and grabbed the League of Losers badges from his pocket.

He looked at each of his friends: Mona, Sheila, Tony and Bryan. They were always ready for a new midnight adventure and always had each other's backs. Bram put on his evilest smile, looked his friends in the eyes and said, 'Are you all ready to become losers?'

ACKNOWLEDGEMENTS

And then there were three! I'm so happy that we're on the third Villains Academy book, with more crazy antics and a cast of fabulous new characters. I will never tire of writing about these villains' adventures, so my biggest thank you goes to all you readers, young and old, for following the Cereal Killers (and me) through this crazy world.

As always, my next thank you goes to my wonderful agent and the first villain to ever enter the doors of Villains Academy – Lydia. My favourite evil mastermind and the best champion I could ever wish for.

Thank you to the evil geniuses at S&S for allowing me to bring these stories to life. To my fabulous editors, Amina and Ali – and more recently, Carla, for enrolling at Villains Academy. Thank you for helping me push my imagination and words even further. To Sean, Rachel, Laura, Ellen, Dan, Dani, Leena and everyone behind the scenes at S&S towers – THANK YOU for your expertise and kindness (Master Mardybum would be cursing you all).

Thank you to my family for your undying

support. To Mum, Dad, Jamie, Luke, Nicola, Brad, Gracie, Caron, Martin, Jim, Maureen, Jaxon and Alfonso. You all make me slightly crazier every day, which feeds into the madness that I write down, so thank you.

A special thank you to my partner in crime, Mitch, who this book is dedicated to. Sorry you had to wait until book three for a dedication, but I hope it was worth the wait. Love you lots.

Thank you to my friends, who big me up, keep me sane and make me celebrate every small achievement. To Emily, Anna, Hannah, Sarah, Sam, Lins, Seb, Sarah L, Lois, Asmaa and Leah. And of course, Nicola B, my No. 1 fan.

A huge thank you to the booksellers, bloggers, teachers and librarians I've met over the past year. You are all so kind and generous and I feel very lucky to have shared my journey with you. A special shoutout to Karen (Wallee), Tom Griffiths, Chloe at my local Waterstones and to Helen at Wonderland Bookshop for being so badass.

The Gruesome Games wouldn't have been what they are without the incredible kids I've met at my school events. Thank you, Mason, who I met on my first-ever school event at Bexleyheath school. Your enthusiasm stuck with me for months and I was *obsessed* with the evil sandwich character that you created – Master Masonnaise is dedicated to you. I hope you enjoyed him and keep creating your own characters. I know one day I will be reading your books. And thank you to Amelia, the winner of the National Book Tokens competition with your fabulous character, Lightning Lily – I hope you enjoyed her brief appearance.

Thank you to my fellow authors, illustrators and the 2023 debut group. I love being part of your bookish community; you are truly the best bunch of people!

Thank you to Sheila the real-life ghost. Please stop tickling my feet.

And my final thank you goes to the Cereal Killers. To my bunch of misfits and weirdos. I love writing about you and you will always remind me to embrace myself and badness. Thank you for saving me and changing my life.

WHO IS
RYAN HAMMOND?

Ryan Hammond is an author, illustrator and book designer. He likes quirky characters, nature and VILLAINOUS streaks.

He currently lives in Sheffield in an extremely haunted house, surrounded by lots and LOTS of books. *Villains Academy* was his first book.

HOW TO DRAW BRAM

1.
Draw a circle.

2.
Add ears.

3.
Add eyes, a nose
and a mouth.

4.
Add the swirls of
Bram's hair.

5.
Add strands of hair
below the swirls.

6.
Add fur all over.

7.
Draw a body
and arms.

8.
Add legs, feet
and hands.

9.
Colour in for a woolly
jumper effect!

HOW TO DRAW MONA

1.

Draw a circle.

2.

Draw two smaller circles for eyes.

3.

Add pupils, eyelids, a nose and mouth.

4.

Draw ears and add earrings.

5.

Add fringe.

6.

Draw an oval for the top of Mona's hat.

7.

Draw the point of her hat and 'GO AWAY' badge.

8.

Add body.

9.

Draw her arms crossed.

10.

Add legs, feet and long hair.

11.

Colour in for extra grumpiness!

HOW TO DRAW BRYAN

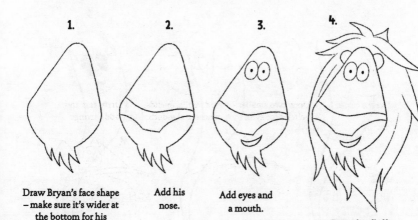

1. Draw Bryan's face shape – make sure it's wider at the bottom for his furry chin.

2. Add his nose.

3. Add eyes and a mouth.

4. Draw his fluffy mane.

5. Draw his front legs and arch of his back.

6. Add his back legs so he's sitting down.

7. Add his tail and colour in – don't forget his furry texture!

HOW TO DRAW SHEILA (X2)

1.

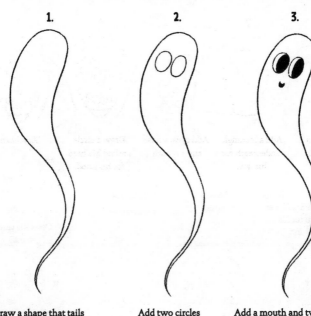

Draw a shape that tails off – any shape, Sheila is really flexible!

2.

Add two circles for eyes.

3.

Add a mouth and two smaller circles inside the first two to give her the hollow-eye look!

1.

Draw a shape that tails off – any shape, Sheila is really flexible!

2.

Add two circles for eyes.

3.

Add a mouth and two smaller circles inside the first two to give her the hollow-eye look!

HOW TO DRAW TONY

1.

Draw a circle.

2.

Add a rectangle underneath for his jaw.

3.

Add eyes, a nose and a mouth.

4.

Draw a circle around his head for his hood.

5.

Add horns!

6.

Draw the front two strands of his cape, add a button and his 'Le Bone' badge.

7.

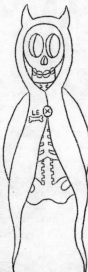

Add his arms, ribs and hips.

8.

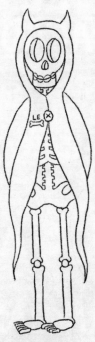

Draw his legs and feet – remember they are bones!

9.

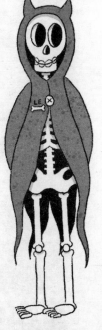

Colour in for extra spookiness!

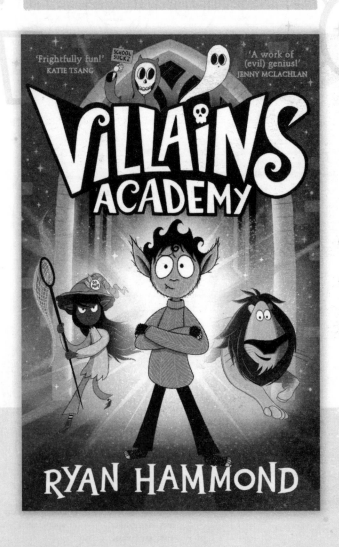

OR CAN YOU TAKE DOWN AN EVIL SUPER VILLAIN IN THE SECOND BOOK?

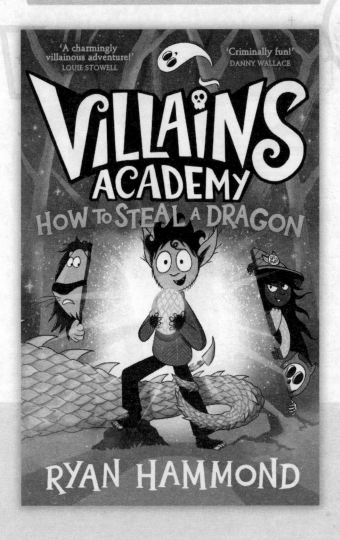

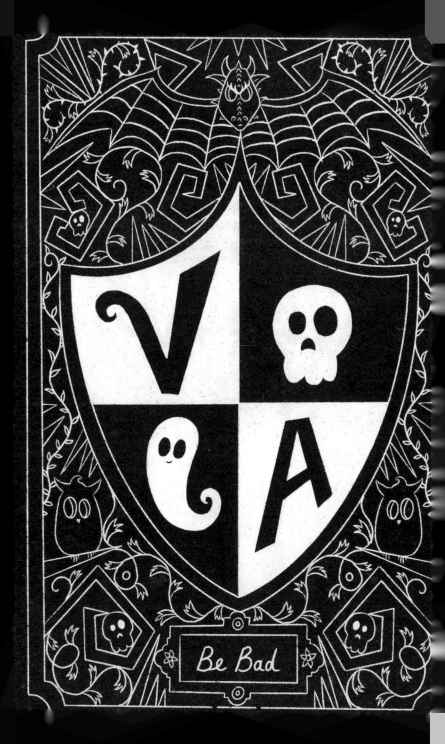

Be Bad